FLORIDA
FIREFIGHT

FLORIDA FIREFIGHT

RANDY WAYNE
WHITE

WRITING AS CARL RAMM

OPEN ROAD

INTEGRATED MEDIA

NEW YORK

Cover design by Andy Ross

978-1-5040-3514-9

This edition published in 2016 by Open Road Integrated Media, Inc.
180 Maiden Lane
New York, NY 10038
www.openroadmedia.com

FLORIDA FIREFIGHT

ONE

Only minutes before he lifted the sniper rifle and took the shot that would end his career as a Chicago cop—and force him to become America's deadliest vigilante—James Hawker adjusted his climbing belt, cradled his weapon and flipped out the little pocket transceiver.

"SWAT One to Ground Leader. Copy?"

The transceiver crackled.

"Yeah, what's up, Hawker—besides yourself, I mean." It was a rare attempt at humor for Captain Boone Chezick, and his laugh sounded like grinding glass.

Hawker was seventeen stories high, strapped to window-washer bollards on the outside of the Fidelity Insurance Building.

He wore a black oilskin sweater and black watch cap.

A bleak November wind pounded across Lake Michigan, ricocheting around the cement and stone canyons of downtown Chicago. South, toward Lake Shore Drive, the Playboy Club beacon scanned the night, as if seeking Jap Zeros from some 1940s war movie. The Sears Tower—the tallest building in the world—and the twin towers of the Hancock Building loomed above the city, bathed in piercing light.

3

"Our boy's getting nervous, Chezick," Hawker said softly. The rubber antenna of the transceiver was frigid against his cheek. Hawker flexed his fingers, trying to work away the cold and stiffness. "He's got all twelve kids lined against the north wall of the room. He's been pacing back and forth, swinging that .357 stainless around. The telephone is on a desk in the west corner of the room. Every time he goes to the phone to negotiate with the governor, I get about a second-and-a-half look at his face, free and clear."

"So?"

"So give me the shot, Chezick."

"What, the great James Hawker is finally asking permission to kill?" There was another hack of laughter. "Maybe that private warning you got from the police superintendent made it through your thick Irish skull, huh?"

Hawker willed his voice to remain calm, and it came out a hoarse whisper. "Chezick, those hostages in there are kids. Maybe fourteen or fifteen—about the same age I was when old Ed knocked you on your ass for trying to force payoff money on him. That was twenty years ago, so let's cut the crap, huh? You hated my dad; you don't like me and, to tell the truth, I'm not going to be inviting you on any canoe trips—but that's all personal. This is business, Chezick. You're a good enough cop to know the difference. We've got a crazy Guatemalan locked in a room with a bunch of rich school kids, and I want permission to put him away."

The entire time he spoke, Hawker's eyes never left the seventeenth-floor window of the building across West Webster Street that held kidnapper and hostages.

4

"And I'm telling you, Chezick, if you make me wait too long again, and someone dies because I don't take the shot when I have it—"

"You've got your orders, Hawker," Boone Chezick said firmly, but his voice had changed. It was tinged strangely with regret. For the first time he sounded almost human. "And those orders come straight from the superintendent, and the superintendent is getting his orders from a hell of a lot higher than that." He cleared his throat, almost as if embarrassed. "It's a political thing, Hawker. It's an election year, and a certain public official likes the idea of all the free national coverage. They've got enough footage of him in sincere negotiations with that Guatemalan to make you gag—and the son of a bitch doesn't speak a word of Spanish. But that asshole up there with the .357 is a natural Dan Rather subject, and this politician doesn't want you blowing away his meal ticket—"

"*Oh, shit.*"

"So those are your orders, Hawker. You've got a rep for playing it close and acting on your own. I know you got some bum orders the last time you were in this situation, and we've all had bad luck—"

Bad luck, my ass, thought Hawker. *A man and four women died the last time I followed orders and waited.*

"But not this time," Chezick continued. "The superintendent says to tell you personally that if you fire without permission, it's immediate suspension—no questions, no excuses. From that distance, shooting through glass, there's too much chance of your hitting one of the kids. That's exactly the kind of coverage the politicians don't need. Also, if one of the kids dies because you don't take out the Guatemalan with your first shot, you're off the force—and in jail. Because you can be goddamn sure our elected officials are not going to take the rap."

"And what if he opens fire first?"

"The interpreter says the kidnapper sounds pretty stable. Says he's under control. All he wants is a million in cash and an air ticket home—everything but Dolly Parton's tits. Don't worry—if things start to go sour, the negotiating team will sense it and give you the word."

"*Right.*"

"And Hawk"—Chezick was suddenly awkward—"if it was up to me, that goat fucker woulda been dead fifteen minutes ago when you got your first clear look at him, and we'd all be on our way home. Your old man and me may not have been best buddies, but I respected the hell out of him. And I was as sorry as anybody on the force when those two sleazy punks put him away. God help them if a member of the Chicago PD ever finds them."

It hadn't been easy for Chezick to say, and Hawker thanked him. He signed off after making sure the other four men on his SWAT team had heard the orders, then settled back against his climbing belt, legs braced against the stone wall of the Fidelity Building.

The wind was gusting now, and he could smell the stink of the lake and the industrial stench of the city.

Below him miniature squad cars threw bursts of blue light across roadblock gates, and miniature people stood in groups, braced against the cold. Men shouldering television news cameras and young women carrying microphones hustled from group to group, hoping to squeeze out every last juicy detail.

Hawker knew the news people, and he liked most of them. But he also knew that to them, the difference between a local story and the chance to be picked up by their New York affiliate was death. A cop's death. A kid's death. A kidnapper's death. It didn't matter. It took a lot of death and misery to pay for Dan's penthouse or Walter's wardrobe.

He wondered if they slept well at night.

Movement across Webster Street caught his attention. He lifted his rifle and had a look. The rifle was a Remington 700, military issue, which meant it had a dull finish. Its five-round magazine held NATO 7.62 caliber ammunition, which produced a muzzle velocity of 850 meters a second. Effective range was close to a half mile. Atop the weapon was fitted a massive Star-Tron Mark 303a night vision scope. It had a 135 millimeter f16 lens, which worked on a light intensification system. All available light—from moon, stars, streetlights—was collected by the objective lens, then focused onto an intensifier tube, where the light was amplified some fifty thousand times.

The Guatemalan kidnapper had kept his stronghold in almost total darkness. But when Hawker sighted in, focusing carefully, the room across the street was bathed in amber daylight.

As usual, the kidnapper was out of view, but the twelve kids still stood in a line, backs to the wall.

Hawker fingered the safety to be certain it was on.

The Star-Tron made it seem as if he were in the room with them.

One by one he scanned the teenage faces. Two of the five boys had been crying; their eyes were puffy. The faces of the seven girls displayed various degrees of shock. The white designer slacks of the prettiest girl—a tawny-haired adolescent

7

with the body of a twenty-year-old—showed a dark funneling stain at the crotch. She had wet herself, presumably when the Guatemalan had first threatened them with his .357.

Hawker sighed, disgusted. They were all students at the most exclusive private school in Chicago: Sherwood Anderson Prep. It was more expensive than Latin Private—which once had asked applicants for their bank account numbers—and even more liberal than Francis W. Parker School, which was a bastion of the noble and naive left-wing politics so chic among the very rich and the very spoiled.

Somehow these kids had become associated with the Guatemalan—probably through a student whose father had once been a South American embassy official. The Guatemalan was some kind of ultra left-wing political outlaw, and the chance to offer him help was just too romantic for the dumb little bastards to pass up.

Now they were paying a big price for it.

The climbing belt cut into Hawker's back, and the cold wind sieved through the oiled wool sweater.

He kept the Remington 700 sighted on the window across the street: ready, waiting. He had his orders, and reluctantly he would follow them.

Something Chezick had said touched one of his memory electrodes.

"I was as sorry as anybody on the force when those two sleazy punks put your dad away. God help them if a member of the Chicago PD ever finds them."

It was more than five years ago that the two amateur thieves, by taking him by surprise from behind, had killed his father; the father who had raised him, instructed him and inspired him to follow in his footsteps to the Chicago PD. Working alone, Hawker had tracked the bastards down within twenty-four hours of the murder—before the homicide squad assigned to the case had even gotten started.

And Detective Lieutenant James Hawker knew that if the killers were ever found again, it would be a piece at a time, in some very deep, very cold water.

7:39 P.M.

Rigaberto Laca, a lieutenant in the Guatemalan left-wing guerrilla Tigre squad, felt a terrible roaring in his head, and his heart pounded high in his throat. If he was to die, he knew he must take as many Americans with him as possible.

It was all for the cause. He felt a religious thrill move through him. Yes, that was it—for the cause. He would become a martyr, a hero of his people, mourned by politicians and generals alike.

But why must he die? His brain scanned frantically for another answer. Wouldn't the million dollars, which he had demanded as "American War Tax," be just as helpful to the cause? That had already been promised him, to be paid by the rich father of the blond-haired boy who now stood with the others against the wall.

He was a defiant one, this blond boy. He had not cried like the others, and he had not begged. This boy the others called Jake was the one who had discovered that his classmates were secretly hiding and helping the Guatemalan. He was the one who had notified the authorities, then come to warn his classmates.

He was the cause of it all, and to Rigaberto Laca, he symbolized all rich and aloof white Americans—everything he despised about this country.

We shall see how brave you are, he thought. *We shall see.*

The pressure in his head grew worse, and he wiped the sweat from his mahogany-color face, slinging it at the blond boy. The boy did not flinch. The Guatemalan trembled with his hatred. Once again the girl with the yellow hair and large breasts began to sob.

"*Cesá!*" he yelled at her. He was sick of her squalling, for it made the awful roaring in his head worse. "*Vamos, cesá!*" He waved the .357 magnum with its scalpel-color barrel at her, and she began to cry louder. "Hey! *Puta!*"

Forgetting about the window, he switched on the light. He walked toward the girl, a wild look in his eyes, all the while thinking: *Guillermo, why have you not telephoned? You are a diplomat; you are part of all this—yet you have not come forth and demanded immunity for me. Always it is that American politician who promises, promises, promises. But I know the pigs will kill me the moment I walk from this room. The Americans are weak; the Americans are pigs, and they have no honor. Guillermo, why have you forsaken me. . . .*

7:44 P.M.

Someone had flicked on a light.

James Hawker tensed as he watched the Guatemalan suddenly appear in the window, revolver leveled, dark face soaked with sweat.

Hawker instinctively brought the cross hairs of the Star-Tron night vision scope to bear on the side of the kidnapper's head.

With his left arm wrapped through the sling, bracing the Remington, Hawker grabbed the transceiver in his right hand and began to speak. He didn't take his eye from the scope.

"Chezick! He's moving. Something's wrong. One of the girls in there is crying. Damn it, Chezick, let me have him!"

"Hold it, Hawker! Let me check! They're calling him now; it'll divert his attention. Don't fire yet, damn it! Do you read me? Acknowledge, Hawker. Acknowledge, damn it!"

Coldly and steadily, James Hawker clicked off the safety of his sniper rifle and took aim, sighting in on the base of the dark man's skull.

At that very instant the Guatemalan disappeared from the window, drawn to the telephone.

7:45 P.M.

Later the interpreter working for the Chicago Police Department would realize that the seeming gibberish the kidnapper, Rigaberto Laca, had shouted at him in their final telephone conversation was really a combination of political slogans interspersed with a single unexplained name: *Guillermo*.

Not sensing how desperate the situation had suddenly become, the negotiating team still didn't turn Hawker loose.

When the Guatemalan finally threw down the phone with a choking cry of "Death to Americans!" he turned on the dozen frightened teenagers against the wall.

They saw the new look on his face, and several more of them began to sob softly. Laca found himself about to step in front of the room's single window, then thought better of it. He decided he would kill as many as he could where they stood, then turn the gun on himself rather than die at the hands of one of the pigs.

A horrific grin froze his face as he lifted the .357 and drew the hammer back.

He had decided to kill the blond boy, Jake, first. But, unexpectedly, the yellow-haired girl with the big bosom gave a piercing scream and bolted for the door.

The Guatemalan grabbed her with his left hand and hauled her back. His laughter was like the scream of a hyena. With a jerk he ripped her blouse away, scattering buttons across the linoleum. She tried to cover her heavy breasts with her arms, but he slapped the arms away and began to squeeze her hard, the knuckles of his left hand white with effort.

"You bastard—let her go!"

The Guatemalan didn't see blond-haired Jake coming. The kid shoulder tackled him high, like a linebacker hitting a dummy. The kidnapper stumbled toward the middle of the room, squeezing off three deafening shots.

Jake's chest exploded, the impact slamming him against the wall.

The second shot severed the girl's right wrist.

The third shot caught her low in the abdomen, and she spun dead on the floor.

The remaining ten teenagers were frozen, already deep in shock. A chubby sixteen-year-old boy was on his knees, praying incoherently. Someone was crying for her mother, over and over and over again.

The kidnapper, with blood splattered over him and the horrific grin still fixed on his face, took two slow steps toward them. He lifted the .357, pulled the hammer back, and Rigaberto Laca was just about to fire when splintering glass crashed to the floor—and the Guatemalan's head disappeared.

The corpse took two hesitant steps, as if unsure what had happened.

The headless creature collapsed on the linoleum then, jugular pumping.

7:48 P.M.

Lieutenant Detective James Hawker ejected the spent cartridge jacket and slammed the bolt of the Remington closed.

Through the Star-Tron scope, he could see the body of the teenage girl, her face strangely peaceful. Beside her was the brave, hard-nosed kid who had tried to save her.

The Guatemalan lay in the middle of the floor in a lake of blood.

"You son of a bitch," Hawker whispered. "You lunatic son of a bitch."

From the transceiver in his pocket came the voice of Captain Boone Chezick. "Ground Control to SWAT One. Hawk? I think permission to fire will be coming soon. But play it safe, damn it—pass it on to your team. The interpreter says the Guatemalan is starting to sound a little crazy, and someone has already reported hearing shots. You got that, Hawker?"

Hawker reached into his pocket and switched off the radio.

TWO

Two weeks later Hawker awoke just after dawn in his bachelor flat. Alone.

Outside snow swirled past the second-floor window in the gray light. He realized what day it was, and he wondered: *Where do the unemployed go for Thanksgiving in Chicago?*

Downstairs his Scottish landlady, the widow Hudson, rattled pots and pans. There was the smell of coffee boiling.

Hawker forced himself from the warm bed and began his morning calisthenics: push-ups, sit-ups and stretching before the morning run. At thirty-four, Hawker was in good shape—but he had to work at it. He hadn't changed that much physically since he'd played football for Kelly High in Chicago, or his two seasons of class-A baseball in Florida for the Tigers organization. He was six-one, just under two hundred. His hair was copper color, and he had a face that his ex-wife once told him was handsome "in a rough and funny sort of way."

His nose looked as if it had been broken more than once—which it had.

Hawker had just pulled on his sweat pants and blue running shoes when the widow Hudson tapped at his door.

"Lieutenant Hawker? Would you be awake this early?"

His landlady was a doughy, fresh-cheeked woman with a lilt in her voice. She did her best to mother him, seeing that he had a "proper break-of-fast," as she called it. Even so, Hawker winced when she continued to call him by the rank he no longer held.

He swung open the door, smiling. "Sure and if it isn't Miz Hudson," he said, imitating her Scottish brogue. "You must be in an awful sweat to get to your gambling agent. Are the ponies in Miami running early this morning?"

She laughed girlishly and shoved a stoneware mug of coffee in his hands. "Not a-tall, not a-tall." Her face was red, and she gave him a conspirator's wink. "But I did win a wee bit yesterday betting on the kickball games."

"Kickball?"

She thought for a moment; then her face brightened. "*Football*. Aye, it was football I won me money on."

"Hah!" Hawker wrapped his arm around her and gave her a quick squeeze. "Then you'll be having every Irish bachelor on Archer Street over for a fine big turkey—myself included, I hope."

She slapped at him, redder yet. "But that's why I knocked you up so early, Lieutenant. You have another invitation. A messenger boy just brought this to the front door." She pulled a note from her apron and handed it to Hawker.

Mr. Hawker:
    It seems we will both be without family for the holiday, so I wonder if you would like to join me at Hayes Hill for din-

ner? Also I would like to discuss with you matters that may
be of great mutual interest. RSVP the enclosed number.

Jacob Montgomery Hayes

It didn't take Hawker long to make the connection. Jake Hayes was the blond kid who had been murdered by the Guatemalan. Jacob Montgomery Hayes was his multimillionaire father.

Hawker thanked the widow Hudson, then went for his run. He jogged through the bleak Chicago morning, his breath fogging and disappearing in the soft storm of snowflakes. He passed St. Barbara High School and disappeared into the winter trees of McGuane Park. For the thousandth time he went over the events that had caused him, a second-generation Chicago cop, to resign.

The police superintendent, committed to Hawker's suspension if he fired without orders, had followed through—but only after the big-wheel politician involved had whined to the press that it wasn't *his* fault the two kids had died. Maybe it was because that trigger-happy cop had opened fire too soon. That was bullshit, of course, but the news people had bought it long enough to make Hawker's suspension imperative. The headlines had hurt the worst: HERO COP MAY HAVE CAUSED KILLINGS.

The superintendent had laid it on the line. "Hawker, Captain Chezick says I should be giving you another medal instead of suspending you. But I don't have much choice. You didn't play by our rules, so you left all of us wide open to criticism from every bleeding-heart politician and liberal who wants to be quoted in the press. You're off the force for two weeks, Hawker. And when you come back, you'll be going on Vice. And you'll follow orders, and you'll keep your nose clean, damn it! That's all."

When Hawker hadn't obediently about-faced and disappeared, the superintendent had looked up from his work. "Anything else?"

Slowly, deliberately, Hawker had pulled out his billfold and removed his badge. "Yeah," he had said, "there is something else." He tossed the spinning badge onto the superintendent's desk. "This."

THREE

So now what would he do? Hawker jogged on, thinking. He had spent the last two weeks holed up, trying to sort it all out. In one way or another he had lived his whole life preparing to be a cop. He had grown up tough in Bridgeport, the Irish section of Chicago, and he and his father, Ed, had watched with disgust as that section changed from a close-knit community to an area ravaged by interlopers who made their living through violent crime.

When the crime got so bad that the understaffed police force couldn't handle it, Ed organized the community into a Neighborhood Watch force—and James Hawker, just a kid, helped. Old Ed had been a master of strategy and was born with the gift of gab. The community rallied behind him. And then a funny thing happened: People who had felt alone in the face of hoods and strong-arm crooks suddenly found strength in their friends and neighbors. People who were terrified of walking the streets at night suddenly found courage in the knowledge of their union.

Old Ed's methods were rough—and not always legal. But they worked.

Crime in the neighborhood was cut to half, and the Neighborhood Watch program spread.

So Hawker had grown up hating the scum who made the lives of the common workaday citizens miserable. People who lived in fear were not happy people. And Hawker had spent his life fighting the bastards and the bullies, the killers and the crooks who preyed on the innocent. He had become a cop, and a damn good cop. And he had planned to carry on the fight.

But how can you fight when you're no longer part of the fighting structure?

Hawker toyed with the idea of applying to the New York or L.A. police departments for a job—but it would just mean more of the same. More restraint; more innocent people dying because the police department, bowing to political pressure, wouldn't allow him to Hawk it. Also, more bureaucratic bullshit; more arrests to be thrown out of court on legal technicalities; more scum set free by lawyers who cared nothing for truth or justice, only the big fees and the proliferation of a legal system that favored the criminal and made them rich in the process.

Hawker, who collected trivia the way some people collected stamps, remembered something he had read: Nearly 60 percent of the people who flunked out of medical school or doctorate programs went into law.

The legal system, it seemed—like too many public school systems—was being run by people without the talent to do anything else. And the politicians were worse.

Even though it was cold, Hawker was working up a good

sweat. Instead of running his usual three miles, he decided to stretch it to five and build up a good appetite for the mysterious dinner with Jacob Montgomery Hayes. Hayes, oddly enough, was the only one who had come to his defense after the shootings. When he was interviewed, Hayes had called the politician involved a naive idiot for trying to bargain with the Guatemalan, and he had praised Hawker for acting without orders. "People in this city ought to get down on their knees and thank God for tough cops like Lieutenant Hawker, who know how to judge the risks and will put their careers on the line to save lives. If Hawker hadn't acted, we would be mourning twelve dead kids instead of two."

Hawker had dropped Hayes a simple note thanking him and telling him his son Jake had died trying to save the life of the girl.

He had heard nothing more. Until now.

As Hawker jogged down Halsted Court, planning to swing southwest on Archer and back home, he suddenly decided to cut through Peoria Green, a large park with woods and grass too often inhabited by drug addicts and muggers. He had seen three rough-looking guys in their late teens or early twenties enter the park, and his cop instincts told him to follow.

He was glad he did.

The three punks had seen something in the park Hawker hadn't: an older, prosperous-looking couple on a morning walk. They must have been in their late sixties, but they were holding hands like high school sweethearts.

The punks brushed passed them, knocking the woman down on the slippery grass. The old man sputtered and raised his fists as if to fight them. But then he seemed to remember he was closer to seventy than twenty-seven, and he went meekly to his wife's aid.

It was pathetic to watch.

One of the punks kicked him as he bent over, and the man fell on his face. Another harassed the woman, kicking her legs out every time she tried to get to her feet. The woman was shocked and in tears, and the kid was laughing. "What'sa matter, you old whore; you clumsy or something, bitch?"

Hawker got there just as they slid the old man's wallet from his pants. When the punks saw him coming, they stood shoulder to shoulder in a show of strength.

"What'cha think you doing, motherfucker? You best get your sorry ass out of here before we slap that fucking smile off your face."

Still running, still smiling, Hawker charged the biggest one. It froze the three of them for an instant, and Hawker veered at the last moment and hit one of the other punks with a straight right that split his face and sent him unconscious to the ground.

He turned to the biggest of them. "I'm still smiling, asshole," he hissed.

The two punks began to back away, holding their hands out. "Hey, man, we was just shitting around. Didn't mean no harm . . ."

Hawker grabbed the mouthy one by the shirt collar and slammed him into a tree. When the kid tried to fight back, Hawker buried his fist in his solar plexus.

His partner disappeared into the trees like a frightened dog.

"You like to kick old folks in the butt, hey, asshole?" Hawker whispered, nose to nose with him. "Well, let's just see how much you like it."

"What'cha mean, mister—"

The old man had helped his wife to her feet, and the two stood in the light snow watching. They looked broken and embarrassed and defeated.

"Sir?" Hawker called. "Would you mind stepping over here for a second?"

The old man released his wife's hand and came reluctantly. Hawker smiled at him. "Sir, I have a feeling you could have taught these creeps a lesson or two a few years ago, and I'm just wondering if you wouldn't mind helping me out now."

The self-esteem flushed back into the man's face, and his shoulders squared slightly. "If I can help . . . if you think I'm able—"

Hawker laughed. "Oh, I'm sure you're able. I recognize an ex-lineman when I see one. No matter how old. And you've got that look—a tackle?"

The man brightened. "Center! A passing center, back when a center had to know what he was doing. But that was forty . . . forty-five years ago."

"Great. Just move over there to the walk where it's not so slippery." As the old man strode away, Hawker tightened his grip on the punk. "Listen and listen good, asshole," he said softly. "You're going to let that old fellow kick your butt around this park—"

"Like fuck I am—"

Hawker's hand slid from the shirt collar to the punk's throat. He began to squeeze. "Nod your head when you change your mind."

The punk nodded immediately. "That's better," said Hawker. "And one last thing: I've lived in this town most my life, and I know everybody there is to know. If I ever hear of those two folks being hurt by you or anybody else, I'm going to come after you. You and only you. And I'll hunt you down like a dog. Now walk out there and bend over."

The old man's first kick was tentative, but he soon got the hang of it. Before long the punk was sent sliding on his face with every boot. The old man was grinning like a kid. "Mildred!" he called to his wife. "Why don't you come over here and give this rascal a swift one!"

His wife dismissed the offer with a wave. "No, Frankie, you go ahead and have your fun. But we have to be going soon, don't forget. The grandkids will be here for Thanksgiving." The woman turned to Hawker then, and her smile was warm and filled with gratitude. "Thank you," she said softly. "Thank you for giving back to my husband what he treasures most—his dignity."

Hawker nodded and winked at her.

"You're a police officer, aren't you," she said after studying him for a moment. It was a statement, not a question. Somehow people always knew.

Hawker began to nod but caught himself. He shrugged. "No, ma'am, I'm not. I'm just a private citizen . . . like you."

FOUR

Hayes Hill was a sprawling estate on Lake Michigan located in Kenilworth, Chicago's wealthiest suburb. A black wrought-iron fence and an electronic security gate protected the grounds.

Hawker arrived at the appointed time, and the gate swung open as if it had eyes. He drove through in the vintage midnight-blue Stingray he had bought at police auction and then had tenderly restored by a mechanic friend of his.

It was late afternoon, and a gray wind blew off the lake. The sky was leaden, with no sign of the sun, and Hawker could see the Hayes house through a forest of bare trees.

It was a stone fortress, museum-size, built in the Prairie House style of Frank Lloyd Wright. Ivy-covered walls. Greenhouses with fogged windows. Marble fountains clogged with winter leaves. It looked like the whole estate had gone into mourning for summers past. Or for a dead boy.

As Hawker made the turn into the drive, the gate swung closed behind him.

After his run Hawker had become increasingly curious about

the invitation from Jacob Montgomery Hayes. It was unlikely he would invite a stranger to Thanksgiving dinner out of loneliness. And the statement on the invitation—"It seems we will both be without family for the holiday"—indicated Hayes had done at least some superficial checking into Hawker's life.

So Hawker had done some checking of his own.

Hawker was no big spender—couldn't afford to be. Also he believed that the more things a man owns, the more he *is* owned. When he did buy, he bought carefully: clothes, books, car; and buying carefully usually meant buying the very best available. But Hawker's one big personal indulgence was a 128K RAM computer, complete with two disk drives, telephone modem and printer. He had reasoned it would come in handy for police work, and he was right; it had proved invaluable.

Timothy Hoffacker, a computer-whiz friend of his, had talked Hawker into buying it. Hawker had a natural dislike and distrust for modern "conveniences," but Timothy was convincing. He had listed all the advantages a computer would give Hawker and noted all the time it would save. Hawker believed him because he knew Timothy was unsurpassed in his field; only two years before Hawker had had to arrest him on a computer-bank pirating scheme that was so brilliantly conceived that the company had decided to hire him rather than press charges.

Hawker bought a computer and, red-faced with triumph, Timothy had presented him with an outlaw collection of software that would allow Hawker to steal data from just about any computer on earth that was serviced by a telephone company.

So when Hawker decided to check out Jacob Montgomery Hayes, he did it from the comfort of his own small study. Boot-ing his unit with one of Hoffacker's outlaw disks, he dialed a special number in City Hall, then fixed the phone in the telephone modem. Back in the late sixties, a Chicago PD unit called the Red Squad, a CIA-type organization, had put together in-depth files on just about every person of note in the city. Public outrage had rendered the Red Squad all but impotent, but the files remained.

Hawker had punched in the proper control commands, and soon his computer was probing the city's computers, seeking to unlock their entry codes through a program method Timothy called Random Ultraspeed Taps on Locked Entry Data.

The name was a mouthful, but it worked. And it had an appropriate acronym: RUSTLED.

His computer had beeped and flashed, scanning. When the proper path name was discovered, the life of Jacob Montgomery Hayes began to roll across his video screen in luminescent green letters. The Red Squad had done its research. The report was in excess of five thousand words, filled with dates, facts, rumors and gossip.

In Hawker's mind it boiled down to this: Hayes was a Texan, born dirt poor. He had gone to work in the oil fields after dropping out of high school. He had worked the rigs by day, and in his own little machine lab at night. Tinkering and inventing were passions. In 1946, at the age of twenty-two, he patented an internal flush-sleeve coupling device that became indispensable to deep oil well drilling. By the age of twenty-five he was a millionaire. He continued tinkering, but his interests expanded into business and investing. His fortune grew proportionately. His portfolio included operations in America, Canada,

Europe and Central America. He lived the life rich bachelors are expected to live.

But in 1967, at the age of forty-three, Hayes suddenly dropped from sight. Apparently he traveled, studied—treating himself to the education he had missed as a youth. He began financing—and joining—research teams on biological and zoological expeditions. He studied Zazen in Japan. Then he dropped totally from sight, and there were rumors of him in deep seclusion at a monastery on Crystal Mountain in Nepal. And then, just as suddenly, he reappeared in Chicago, where his corporate headquarters were based. He resumed control of his dynasty as if nothing had ever happened. He seemed to care little for politics or society. He married a local woman who was known to be a fortune hunter. In 1970 a son was born to them, Jacob, Jr.—Jake. In 1974 his wife died of a cerebral aneurism. He was a member of the Fly Fishing Federation of America and owned some of the top field and retrieving trial dogs in the country.

And that was it.

Hawker had never spoken with the man or met him. Even so, he had an idea it was going to be a very interesting dinner.

FIVE

The butler who let Hawker in looked like a character out of a 1940s English mystery movie. He was saber thin, with a face of marble. His sense of humor was as dry as the tuxedo he wore was expensive.

"James Hawker to see Mr. Hayes."

"How nice."

"He was expecting me at five."

"What a wonderful invention, the Timex."

From the foyer where they stood, Hawker could see a balconied front room and a massive sweeping staircase.

"If he's busy, I wouldn't mind just wandering around the grounds a bit. Looks like your gardener has a passion for exotics."

"Our gardener is a drunk, and his passions are too loathsome to contemplate. If you will, sir, this way."

Hawker followed the butler down a cavernous hallway. Their footsteps echoed. He stopped at a double set of french walnut doors and swung them wide.

"Mr. Hayes sends his compliments of the season and requests you make yourself comfortable here."

The room was done in fine woods and leather. The ceiling was sixteen feet high, and the stone fireplace alone was as big as Hawker's study back in Bridgeport. Bookshelves were stacked clear to the ceiling, and there were glass-enclosed displays of mounted butterflies, spiders and strange-looking insects. At one end of the room, near the fireplace, was a desk with a fly-tying vise. Behind the desk was a huge gun case filled with fine side-by-sides and over-and-unders. On the wall were original oil paintings of braces of Brittany spaniels, yellow labs and a rough and solitary-looking Chesapeake. The only other painting in the room was of a young blond-haired boy: Jake. In the opposite corner of the room was an elevated area covered with Japanese matting. Against the wall was a low shrine on which sat a brass Buddha, a small brass bell and an incense holder. The center of the room was dominated by an ancient chunk of Americana: a huge, hand-hewn oak table. It had been restored and polished to glass.

Hawker decided to try the butler's sense of humor. "The dining room, right?"

The butler's lips curled as if to smile, but only for an instant. "Hardly, sir. This is where Mr. Hayes ties bits of animal hair to fishhooks and performs strange chanting rituals."

"Ah—the living room."

The butler fixed him with a look, as if studying him through bifocals. "It's the library, sir: a place where one's books are kept."

"Hank, are you giving our guest a hard time?"

The butler winced visibly. The figure standing in the doorway was an average-size man in his early sixties. He was balding, wore wire-rimmed glasses and held a heavy briar pipe. He was dressed comfortably in gray slacks and a wine-red smoking jacket. He had a craggy face, as rough hewn as the oak table. But there seemed to be nothing rough about the man himself, as if he had traded his dirt-poor Texas past for a life that was both sophisticated and enlightened. He laughed and held an outstretched hand to Hawker, saying as he did, "Hank's a little cold around the edges, but he's really got a heart of gold—isn't that right, Hank?"

"Hendricks, if you please, sir. We much prefer *Hendricks* to"—he made a face as if he had just touched soiled laundry—"*Hank*."

Jacob Montgomery Hayes hooted. "Hank, tell Gloria Mr. Hawker and I will be taking our Thanksgiving dinner here. Tell her to do it up right. Mr. Hawker spends so much time watching his weight and staying in shape during the rest of the year that I'd bet he's a lot like the rest of us: he looks forward to the holidays so he can finally let himself go at the table."

"Then you won't be having your normal dinner, sir—dried goat cheese, vegetables and green tea?" Hendricks inquired.

Hayes gave another gust of laughter. "Hank likes to make his little jokes about my vegetarian ways, Mr. Hawker. And Hank—bring our guest a beer." He looked at Hawker, raising his eyebrows. "You usually drink those diet beers, but you prefer Tüborg or Guinness, right? Tüborg, Hank. And don't bother with a glass. Mr. Hawker likes it in the bottle."

Hendricks closed the door behind him, and Hayes waved Hawker into one of the leather recliners near the fire. "Hendricks is a good man. Been with me one way or another since 1949. Quite a hero during the Second World War. He was a sergeant major in British M16. Did espionage and counterespionage work out-side the United Kingdom. Hell of an intelligence man. The Russians wanted him—offered him everything but an autographed picture of Stalin. Could have retired with a general's pension by now, but he's a fifth-generation gentleman's gentleman. He's dead-set proper during working hours—except for that wicked sense of humor of his. But once or twice a month we slip off together to fish or hunt, and he becomes my best friend again. He loves bird hunting, and so do I. I love everything about it: the smell of the gun oil and the fields; love to watch those dogs work. But it's hard to rationalize a vegetarian blowing mallards out of the sky. So Hank does the shooting, and I work the dogs." Hayes smiled, and a pair of shrewd brown eyes locked on Hawker. "You see, I'm a hypocrite, Mr. Hawker. We all are, but I'm the worst kind of hypocrite: I realize what I am but go right ahead anyway."

Hawker sat in his chair, watching the fire. He was smiling. It had been done very neatly. In the space of a few sentences, Hayes had told him that his life-style had been personally checked right down to the brand of beer he preferred. That had been impressive enough, but then Hayes had gone on and done what men in the high-powered world of international business never do: revealed a character flaw, served it right up on a tray. But there would be a price, that Hawker knew. Hayes seemed to be saying: let's cut through the bullshit. I'm prepared to be honest with you. You damn well better be honest with me.

Hawker turned to him. "So how did you get your information about me? Private investigation agency?"

"Private eye? Trench coat and cigarette following you through the streets of Chicago?" Hayes smiled. "Hardly."

Hendricks entered with the tray, stone faced. When he left, the older man settled deeper into his chair, feet stretched toward the fire. He said, "Every century has a key word, Mr. Hawker. The seventeenth century was *exploration*, the eighteenth century was *civilization*. The key word for this century will undoubtedly be *datumization*—if you and Mr. Webster will forgive me. Anyone who has achieved any small success in this country has been investigated and categorized by someone somewhere. The most intimate details of our lives can be found in data banks in places that would shock most people. Data has become the new god, Mr. Hawker."

He leaned toward the fire, looking closer at Hawker. "For instance," he went on, "learning the details of your distinguished career was easy. In a relatively short time you compiled more than forty commendations for superior police performance. You are the only person to win both the Lambert Tree Award and the Carter Harrison Award for valor, Chicago's highest honors. You are also an expert marksman, boxer and scuba diver. You became best known for your enterprising methods—not to mention fearlessness—in hostage situations. In 1977 you architected a Chicago Special Weapons Attack Team, trained especially for dealing with such situations. Unfortunately, your growing reputation also brought closer scrutiny. Certain liberal factions in the city didn't like what they thought to be strong-arm methods. Your superiors were told to keep a close eye on you. In March 1982 you killed a kidnapper with what your superiors thought to be a risky shot. You were privately censured and ordered never, under any circumstances, to fire again without orders. In July 1983 your team was faced with another hostage situation. An escapee from a psycho ward had taken—"

"I know the grim details, Mr. Hayes," Hawker said softly, but there was an edge to his voice. "I had a shot but didn't take it because I hadn't received orders yet. And the five hostages—a doctor and four nurses—were slaughtered. That's what all this is about, isn't it? I had three clear chances to shoot before your son, Jake, was murdered, and now you're wondering why in God's name I didn't disobey orders earlier and—"

Hayes waved his hands, interrupting. "No, James, it's not about that at all." The older man sighed, and an infinite weariness showed itself for the first time. "I happen to believe life and death are much the same." He waved absently at the Japanese matting in the corner, as if the smiling little Buddha were explanation enough. "I loved my son as I have never loved anything on this earth; I idolized him. But he is gone now. It's as simple as that. I can accept it, deny it, despise it or go mad with it. But he is gone. Nothing will change that."

"Then why am I here? You didn't invite me just for an informal chat over cranberry sauce. Why the research into my background? Why the offer of honesty?"

Hayes studied him for a moment. "You're an intelligent man, Hawker. And I hope I won't offend you by explaining it all in my own way." He looked at his watch. "Do you want to eat first?"

"No."

Hayes nodded. "Okay. I'll lay it out as briefly as I can." He pointed to the cases of insects he had collected. "I'm an amateur naturalist—"

"A highly respected amateur naturalist," Hawker inserted. Both men smiled. "I did some checking of my own."

"Okay, then: I'm a highly respected amateur naturalist. The

awesome perfection of nature—its design . . . its balance—it's beyond our understanding. But it should never be beyond our acceptance. Nature is perfect. The point cannot even be argued. Try to see all of nature as a single organism. It regenerates, it provides for itself, it adapts to or destroys things alien to its cycles of existence. For instance, there's a tree in South America that would become extinct within a few years were it not for a specialized ant it hosts. The tree provides these ants with everything: special sap for food, special niches to lay their eggs, leaves perfectly designed to provide the ants shelter. In return, the ants never leave the tree—and they utterly destroy any other insect that comes to feed on the tree."

"Mr. Hayes, if I'm supposed to understand this—"

"You will in a moment, Mr. Hawker, I promise." He stuffed his pipe, struck a match and exhaled fragrant smoke. "Our society, when it is healthy, functions like any other organism in nature. It regenerates, it provides for itself and it adapts to or destroys forces that threaten its existence. Unfortunately, though, as you well know, our society is no longer healthy. For some strange reason—complacency, perhaps—it has lost the moral courage to police itself. Because it is necessary to its very survival, nature is sometimes completely and utterly ruthless. Our society has lost that frightening but necessary quality. Murderers are released after a few years to roam the streets again. Rapists are given a few sessions with state-employed psychologists, then sent away to continue their terrorism. If the ants on that tree in South America—or any other organism in nature—were that lax as guardians, their wards would cease to exist." Hayes smacked his fist into his hand. "Extinction—as simple as that. There would be a few generations of biological chaos, then total death. In the same way, Mr. Hawker, our society is slowly but surely dying. I guess you could describe these last twenty years as our period of chaos."

Hayes fiddled with his pipe momentarily. He gave Hawker a meaningful look. "Do you understand what I am saying, Mr. Hawker?"

Hawker did. Although he had never heard it explained so well, he felt the very same way. He nodded.

Hayes's eyes became lasers. "Then be very frank, Mr. Hawker. You know what I'm talking about, and you certainly have some inkling as to the direction this conversation may take. If we continue, are you going to contact one of your police chums and have me arrested for—for—"

"Conspiracy to commit revolution?" Hawker smiled. "If I did, I'm afraid they'd have to take us both away."

Hayes grinned in return. He pressed a button. "Then maybe we should eat as we discuss the problem. Hendricks gets upset if my tsampa gets cold."

For more than an hour the two men talked on. Hawker listened with an ever-growing respect for Jacob Montgomery Hayes. The man was brilliant without being patronizing. He was sincere without being pompous. And when he laughed, it was a good, deep gust—and usually directed at his own shortcomings. Hawker suspected what it was all leading up to, but he finally asked point-blank.

"We've circled the subject too often. How do I fit in?"

Hayes considered the question for a moment, then answered just as frankly.

"It's time society started standing up for itself, James. The courts and the lawyers have swamped themselves with this century's passion: data. They no longer care about right and wrong. They care only for the games they can play by manipulating data. Society is the victim, and it's time the victim started defending itself." Hayes looked him straight in the eye. "I'd like you to help me lead the way. I want you to seek out communities plagued by crime and corrupt people. And, just like in those Neighborhood Watch programs of your dad's, I want you to show the people how to fight back." He paused for a moment while this sank in. "The work will be dirty and thankless. And, as you have no doubt deduced, it will sometimes even be wrong in a legal sense. But it'll be right morally. And morality is the only true governor of any society."

"And I'd be working alone?"

"If you wish. I've made millions, James, and my only heir is dead. When you leave money to charities these days, only about twenty percent of it filters down to those who really need it. I'd like to see something good come of my money, and I can't think of anything more desperately needed by our society. I'll finance everything, buy you any equipment or weaponry you need, send you anyplace you feel it would be helpful to go. I have plenty of connections in high places, and I think you'll find you'll get backing from some surprising sources."

"You have no qualms about violence when necessary?"

Hayes shook his head. "I chose you not only because you're tough enough, but because your record shows you're wise enough to fit the punishment to the crime. If you're dealing with killers, then I fully expect you to kill. As I said, I have connections in high places. If the local law gets onto you, I'll help you in any way I can—but that's no guarantee you won't have to run for your life sometimes. As I said, it'll be a tough and thankless job."

"If I went to work here in Chicago, I wouldn't last a week. The cops know my methods too well. They'd put two and two together."

"I quite agree. That's why I have chosen another state for your first mission. We'll call it an experiment in socio-nature." Hayes shrugged. "If it works, we'll both no doubt be happy, and we can expand the operation. If it doesn't, nothing will be lost."

"I haven't said yes yet."

For a moment Hayes was taken aback. But then he saw Hawker's slow smile, and he took the outstretched hand.

SIX

"A stranger, eh?" The Hispanic man flashed a wicked grin. "We do not like strangers on Mahogany Key." His grin broadened, but no one was laughing. He took a step toward Hawker. "So let me give you some advice, gringo. You put the gas in your fine big car, you pay the nice lady inside, and then you disappear . . ." The man made an exploding motion with his hands. "Pewff!"

The smile was instantly replaced by a brutal glare. "You leave *now*, gringo. Or my friends and me"—the grin returned—"will be forced to cut your pale little ears off and stuff them down your ugly throat!"

The three men behind him roared. They were a seedy-looking bunch, in stained T-shirts and grimy jeans. They all wore sheath knives. In the balmy Everglades air the smell of them was overpowering: a combination of stale cigarette smoke and sour sweat.

It hadn't taken Hawker long to find out why Jacob Montgomery Hayes had sent him to this remote fishing village on the southwest coast of Florida.

Hayes had once made yearly visits to Mahogany Key to fly fish for tarpon. He had stayed regularly at an old and stately hunting and fishing lodge called the Tarpon Inn. Hayes had made friends of the villagers, and he had stayed in touch with many of them. Because he hadn't been able to get to Florida for some time, Hayes hadn't seen fear transform the town.

But one of the villagers had recently called and told him. Hayes's friend, the owner and manager of the Tarpon Inn, had pretended his telephone call was just a holiday exchange of greetings.

But Hayes soon realized it was really a plea for help.

Over the past year more and more Colombians had been moving into Mahogany Key. They flashed a lot of cash and bought all the homes and businesses available.

And then they began to buy homes and businesses that *weren't* for sale, using mobster methods to run many of the honest, hardworking townspeople from the village.

Their reasons for wanting to take over Mahogany Key were soon all too clear. The village was located south of Naples and Everglades City, on Florida's wildest and most remote section of coast. On the seaward side it was guarded by a maze of ten thousand uninhabited mangrove islands. On the landward side it was cut off by the bleak and unforgiving swamps of the Everglades.

There was no place better suited to trafficking in drugs.

And that was exactly what the Colombians were doing—with devastating success. They were making suitcases full of money, and now they were trying to take over the village totally.

Hayes's friend had been given an ultimatum by the

Colombians: sell them the Tarpon Inn or end up a corpse stuck in some 'gator hole in the heart of the Everglades.

Everyone in town was running scared. They had approached their one-man police force—an aging, retired Miami cop—and asked him to seek outside help. But they knew why he couldn't even before they asked: by the time state or federal gears of justice got into motion, the Colombians would have plenty of time for reprisals.

And there were a lot of innocent kids on Mahogany Key.

So Hawker had jetted from the bleakness of a Chicago December into the heat and glare of Miami.

It hadn't taken him long to get ready.

Hayes had made arrangements for Hawker's cover story. Hawker would pretend to be the new owner of the Tarpon Inn. Hayes's friend was more than willing to shed the burden for a while. Hayes had also seen that the equipment Hawker required had been safely shipped ahead.

So Hawker put his Stingray in storage, gave the widow Hudson two months' advance rent, then contacted his ex-wife, Andrea Marie, and told her to spread the word to his friends that he would be out of town awhile. A few years before, the strain of Hawker's passion for dangerous police work had been too much for Andrea, and they had divorced amicably.

Even so they remained close friends—and a little bit in love with each other.

On his last night in Chicago, they had driven outside the city to Lakemoor's Le Vichyssoise, a country French restaurant, for a farewell dinner. Somewhere between the cream of leek soup and the roast duck cooked in wine, the regrets and the desire to take each other to bed again had built until Andrea burst into tears. She was a lithe brunette with a face and body that demanded longing looks from the men in every room she had ever entered. But she also possessed the intimidating demeanor of a woman who knew damn well what she wanted, and contact with those demanding brown eyes of hers usually sent the same men staring away into space, frightened.

"Damn it," she had said, dabbing at the tears with her napkin, "why does a big ugly potato-head like you still affect me this way?"

"That's the trouble with every Jewish-American princess—too emotional."

"Bullshit," she snapped. "It's different between us, you know that. You're an ex-husband, and the modern businesswoman doesn't worry about ex-husbands. She's happy to be free and single—read *Cosmo* or *Ms.* if you don't believe me." The tears began to flow again, and her lips trembled. "So why . . . why do I feel so awful about your . . . *leaving!*" The soft weight of her breasts heaved as she buried her face in the napkin.

Hawker had tried hard not to smile. "People are beginning to stare, woman. And your picture has been in the society sections too often for them not to recognize the famous art gallery owner—"

"Fuck 'em," she cut in.

"My, my, what language!"

She wiped her eyes a last time and gave Hawker a heart-breaking look. "Hawk, you won't tell me why you're going to Florida, but I know it's not just for the sun and surf. You've quit the Chicago force, but I know you too damn well to believe you'll ever give up being a cop." She took his hand and squeezed

41

it gently. For the hundredth—or thousandth?—time, Hawker fought away his sexual wanting for her. "So promise me this," she continued. "Promise me you won't get into trouble down there. And damn well promise me you won't get hurt."

So Hawker had promised. And he had promised again on the way back to her penthouse apartment. And he had promised still again as he forced himself from her bedroom door.

So Hawker had rented a Monte Carlo at Miami International Airport and driven west across the Tamiami Trail, through the scent and heat of the Everglades.

Sun shimmered off the highway, and a sea of grass rolled away toward both horizons, golden as Kansas wheat. The air smelled of citrus and sulfur, and white egrets and grim-looking vultures flushed as he drove. Hawker had found something jazzy and Cuban on the radio, and he hummed along.

It felt good to be alone.

The cold, the politics, the complicated relationships of Chicago all seemed long ago and far away. He felt charged and ready.

Mahogany Key was a village on an island connected to the mainland by a concrete drawbridge. The island was four miles long and three miles wide, with draping ficus trees and coconut palms lining the narrow streets.

The houses were built of wood or block and well maintained, but there was a creeping air of decay about them. It wasn't obvious: a fallen awning that hadn't been replaced, leaf-clogged gutters, abandoned toys in the drives. And the lawns were gradually going to weed. The public park in the tiny downtown area hadn't been mowed in weeks. A wooden dock reeled along the bay side of the island, and fishing shacks built on stilts stood in abandoned clusters out in the shallows. The commercial boats there were wrack-stained and unattended.

Something was obviously very wrong on Mahogany Key.

Hawker cruised slowly over the bridge and into the town. It was Saturday, but most of the businesses were closed.

The few people he saw on the streets caught his eyes briefly, then looked quickly away. They all seemed to walk with their heads down. They seemed in a hurry.

The one business still open was a seedy-looking Shop-and-Go. A flea-ravaged dog slept in the sun in the parking lot near a spilled trash can.

Hawker pulled in for gas and directions.

That was when the four Hispanics converged on him.

And that was when Hawker remembered he had lied to his ex-wife and high school sweetheart, the former Andrea Marie Flishmann.

"You understand, gringo," the Hispanic repeated. "You leave town pronto, or we cut your pretty white ears off, huh?" He was a little shorter than Hawker, heavily muscled, with a Fu Manchu mustache. His grin was a dark scar that showed bad teeth.

Hawker could feel eyes watching from inside the Shop-and-Go: a young mother with a pair of towheaded kids; two beefy-looking middle-aged men with the sun-beaten faces of fishermen; a pretty, Indian-looking woman with long black hair. Their faces were all pressed against the window. Across the street a teenage boy and his father stopped to stare.

Absently Hawker wondered if he could depend on them for help.

But then he saw the look of fear in their eyes, and he knew that he would fight alone.

Theirs were the faces of helplessness, faces he remembered from the Neighborhood Watch days.

He knew he had to give them all a fighting example.

Hawker surprised the Hispanics, taking three quick steps toward Fu Manchu. They stood half an arm's length from each other, face to face. "I'd planned to drive on into Miami this morning," Hawker said, returning the Colombian's grin, "but you know, I've begun to take a real liking to this town. Seems like a real friendly place. Think I'll stick around for a few days."

Fu Manchu flushed, and his eyes darted to his friends. They nodded, ready to help. The Colombian put his hands on his hips, threw back his head and laughed. "This gringo, he is very brave, eh? Very brave and very stupid!" The laugh became a sneer. "I will call you Rojo—it means 'Red'—for your lovely red hair." He gave his three friends a wink. "But remember, Rojo, red is also the color of your blood when it's spilled."

Hawker nonchalantly slid his hands into the oversize military pockets of his British twill guide slacks. "And you're very brave, too—as long as you have these three goons to back you." The Colombian's face described outrage. He stepped as if to swing, but Hawker held up both hands, a sign of momentary truce. "Don't fly off the handle, José—"

"My name is not José!"

"Well, whatever your name is, I'm offering you a fair fight. You and me, José, right here; right now."

"You must think me a fool, gringo—not that I couldn't grind your face to *basura* with one hand."

"Let's just say I'll think you're a coward if you don't try." Hawker smiled and offered a wink of his own. "And so will everyone here."

"Pedro Cartagena is afraid of no man!" the Colombian spat.

"Then why don't you fight him!" It was a woman's voice that interrupted. It was the Indian woman from the Shop-and-Go. She was tall and slim, with a smoky, mystic beauty. Her raven black hair was draped over heavy breasts, and she wore the jeans-and-cotton-knit uniform of college students across the nation. She stood on the step, her face trembling with rage. "I'm so sick of you—you *animals* roaming this town like a pack of dogs, bullying and pushing, that I'd really like to see if you have the courage to fight alone." And when the Colombian didn't immediately react, she seared him with a witting laugh. "It's just as I thought," she said. "You're like all pack animals—cowards when you're by yourself."

The Colombian's eyes were venomous. "Perhaps I will find you alone one night and show you what a coward Pedro Cartagena is," he whispered in a deadly voice. And in the same instant he whirled on Hawker, catching him across the nose with his elbow.

Hawker back-pedaled across the lot, right hand going toward the oversize pockets of his pants in the event all four Hispanics charged him.

They didn't. Hawker wiped the gush of blood away with the back of his hand. This was exactly what he wanted: a public fight, one on one.

Back in Ireland his father had fought the professional circuit to earn the few extra quid it took to keep his wife, son and three daughters fed. He had stuck Hawker in the ring before he was in his teens. First it was the Police Benevolent Boxing Association and then the Golden Gloves.

Every tough kid in the city—Italian, black and Pole—had fought his way in and out of the Archer Boxing Club Gym, and Hawker had slugged it out with all of them.

By the time he was seventeen, Hawker was the Golden Gloves light-heavyweight champion of Illinois. And he had the medals—and the nose—to prove it.

Hawker walked straight at Fu Manchu. People had crowded around them, but the only ones yelling encouragement were the Colombians. The others were frightened to call out—except for the Indian woman. Unafraid, she was openly pulling for Hawker.

Fu Manchu was doing his best imitation of a professional fighter, dancing and bobbing. Hawker slapped the jabs away, waiting for his opening. He didn't have to wait long. Fu Manchu went for the home run punch—a sizzling overhand right. Hawker stepped through it, got Fu Manchu's toes under his left foot, then cracked his face open with a straight right. The Colombian jolted butt first to the asphalt, a look of surprise on his face. He made a motion as if to climb to his feet, but then his glazed eyes rolled back in his head and he collapsed face first on the pavement.

Surprisingly, the other Colombians weren't quick to come to his aid—not with their fists, anyway. Hawker had obviously made an impression. They circled him, glaring, each waiting for the other to make a move. Then, as if they all had the same idea at once, they went for their knives.

SEVEN

Someone screamed as they rushed him. Hawker had no idea who. He was too busy trying to stay alive.

He ducked under the first Colombian and flipped him over his back onto the pavement. The man hit with a massive thud and lay bug-eyed, kicking for oxygen with the wind knocked out of him. In that brief moment of victory, Hawker thought he might actually have a chance.

He was wrong.

Someone hit him from behind immediately. Hawker felt a firelike pain in his left shoulder. He tried to jerk away, but a thick arm was locked around his throat. A fist clubbed him twice on the side of the face, hard. The third Colombian approached him warily, knife vectoring in on Hawker's throat.

"We can't kill him here," insisted the man who was holding him. His voice was thick with nervousness. "Too many eyes here, man. Medelli won't like it."

The name had an effect on the Colombian, and he hesitated for a moment. But just a moment. "After what he did to

Pedro?" The Colombian with the knife spat. "I don't give a shit what Medelli thinks. We cut him now!" He brought the knife back, ready to lunge—and from out of nowhere a beer bottle exploded against the man's face. It threw them off balance just long enough.

Hawker drove his right elbow into the stomach of the man behind him, turned and hit him behind the ear with a chopping right. It didn't put the Colombian down, but it stunned him.

But more important, it finally gave Hawker time to fish the lethal little Walther PPK from the oversize military pocket of his pants. He swung it around, framing each of them in the Walther's U-notch sight.

"You assholes toss those knives away—now!"

The Colombian who had had the wind knocked out of him and Fu Manchu, his face split and covered with blood, got shakily to their feet.

All four slid their sheath knives across the pavement.

Hawker turned to the crowd that had gathered. "One of you folks get to that pay phone and telephone for the law."

They acted as if they were deaf. The men studied their worn hands and kicked at the pavement. The women hung their heads, refusing to meet Hawker's eyes. One by one they turned and slunk away.

Only the pretty Indian girl remained. She flipped her raven black hair back, saying, "There's no law around here, mister. We've got a one-man police force who's too old to be much good and too scared to care." The disgust was razorlike in her voice. "And we've got a bunch of local men who like to guzzle beer and brag about how tough they are—in the safety of their own homes, or the Tarpon Inn bar. But law? You're holding the only law around here, mister."

"Someone tried to help me," Hawker insisted shakily. He was suddenly feeling faint, weak from those shots to the head and loss of blood. One of the Colombians began to edge toward the knives, and Hawker stopped him with a motion of the Walther. "Someone helped a hell of a lot, throwing that bottle."

The Indian seemed to notice his wounds for the first time. Her face paled a little. "Hey, you're hurt. You've been hurt pretty bad." She gave the Colombians wide berth and came to Hawker's side, inspecting him. "That stab wound in your shoulder is pretty deep, and your nose is a mess." She touched his arm wound gingerly. "You said something about being on your way to Miami. Maybe I ought to call an ambulance service over there—"

"No," Hawker said, his voice a whisper. His head was throbbing in the heat, and everything seemed to be coming down a tunnel toward him: noises, sounds, smells; everything. "I'm staying here. I . . . I bought the Tarpon Inn."

"Welcome to Mahogany Key, mister," said the Indian woman as she took his arm, her haunting beauty now a foggy swirl before him. "You're very lucky I'm almost as good at nursing as I am at throwing bottles . . ."

It was the last thing Hawker heard before he fainted.

EIGHT

He awoke to the sound of a teakettle whistling.

Someone was singing: a woman's voice; a ripe, husky alto. The song was "Desperado."

The moon-globe glow of Mahogany Key's old-fashioned streetlights glimmered through a lone window. Starch-white curtains and the prissy vanity and knickknacks of a woman's bedroom caught the pale light of winter dusk in Florida.

Hawker jolted upright in bed, wondering just where in the hell he was. When he moved, his shoulder ached and his head throbbed. He threw back the covers and charged down a hall into what must have been the living room.

Suddenly there was laughter.

"God, what an entrance!" The Indian woman stood behind a modern counter that bordered a small kitchen. She wore a white turtleneck sweater and held a steaming mug in her hand. She studied him for a moment, then nodded her head in comic approval. "I'll give you an eight—" She paused as if in reappraisal. "No, let's make that a nine." She tilted her head, smiling girlishly. "I'm duly impressed, Mr. Whatever-your-name is."

Hawker suddenly realized he was completely naked.

"Shit!"

The woman threw back her head and roared.

"Why in the hell didn't someone . . ." Hawker turned tail and headed back toward the bedroom.

"You shouldn't be running!" she called after him, still laughing. "You'll tear those lovely stitches I sewed!"

A few minutes later Hawker returned, trying his best not to look sheepish. Someone had brought in his duffel bag, and he had changed from the bloody clothes of that afternoon into a pair of light cotton corduroy slacks and a navy blue Shetland crew-neck sweater. After the heat of the day, a cool winter wind blew off the bay.

He took a bar-stool seat at the counter.

The woman put a mug of hot tea in front of him. "Feeling better?" She still wore the wry smile.

"Just great—like someone dumped a quart of vodka down me and dragged me behind a car." Hawker stirred sugar into his tea. "So how did I get here—and what happened to my Hispanic friends?"

"Don't you think introductions are in order first?" the woman asked, chiding him. "After all, I've saved your life, sewed you up, and now I've seen you in all your masculine glory." She gave him a vampish wink. "Pretty nice set of buns there, fella."

"What is it with women today? All that talk of liberation, and you immediately get aggressive."

"Actually, feminist nurses have been slipping Spanish fly

into every little girl's pablum. I know so, 'cause I read it in *Cosmopolitan*."

"Next thing you'll be wanting to fight our wars."

"Personally, I just want to be able to use your bathrooms—or at least see one. Are the toilets *really* different in a men's room?"

They both laughed, and Hawker stuck out his hand. "James Hawker, formerly of Chicago."

Her handshake was firm and dry. "Winnie Tiger, formerly of Buffalo Tiger's Miccosukee Reservation, then the University of Florida, and now good ol' Mahogany Key." She caught Hawker's look and said, "Why the expression of surprise?"

"Well, you have to admit that Winnie seems an unlikely name for an American Indian."

"Crazy Horse and Tecumseh were already taken, so my parents just did the best they could. Besides, my grandmother was a Winnie. She was a Smithsonian anthropologist who came to the 'Glades to study the Miccosukees' pagan mating rituals. Turned out my granddaddy was just the pagan she was looking for." She wrinkled her nose into an evil face. "Old Granddaddy always had a thing for the White-Eyes."

Hawker's chuckle turned into an easy, comfortable laugh. He liked this woman. She was open and bawdy and honest. He saw her closely for the first time. Her beauty was indeed smoky and mystic, and he suspected she had done and seen much in her twenty-five-odd years. She had dark doe eyes and a face like something out of a fashion magazine. Her hair was blue-black in the neon light of the kitchen, and there was a submerged energy about her as if, no matter how much time you spent with her, no matter how well you knew her, you could never see all of her, hold all of her, or understand all of her at once.

It was something in her eyes, some mystery deep and distant and unspoken. Hawker had the sudden impression that if they had met in any other way, it would have taken him months to be allowed past all the little emotional doors she would normally slam in the face of a stranger.

For the first time Hawker didn't mind the beating he had taken at all.

"So what happened to them?"

"My grandparents, or the Colombians?"

"The Colombians."

"My, you do have a one-track mind, don't you." She gave him a sharp look. "You a cop?"

"I just bought the Tarpon Inn, remember? And maybe I'm just worried that if you killed those four goons, I'll have to take the rap for it."

It was supposed to be a joke, but she didn't laugh. Her face grew serious. "I would have, you know—shot them, at least. The looks on their faces . . ." She shuddered, and held her tea mug as if for warmth. "No, I grabbed the gun when you passed out, and they just ran for it. Jumped into their truck and roared off toward the docks."

"Who are they?"

"The Colombians?" There was a bitter edge to her laugh. "Haven't you heard? A bunch of ugly little countries got together a few years ago and decided who would get what part of poor old America. The Arabs got New York and L.A.—'cause of their money, you know. The Japanese got Detroit. The Cubans and

Haitians got Miami. It's a free country, right? Well, the Colombians pulled short straw and were saddled with Mahogany Key." She shuddered again. "We natives aren't too wild about you white folk, but these new interlopers . . . well, they trigger the old gag reflex."

"Do you joke about everything?"

She slid around the counter and took the stool beside Hawker. He could smell the light shampoo odor of her as she hunched over her tea, studying the mug as if it might hold some great truth.

"I tell you, James, people who live here have to joke about it. If they don't, they'll end up crazy with hatred. Or dead. Very, very dead." She locked her brown eyes on his, holding him like an embrace. "Which is what you'll be if you don't get out now. Tonight. They'll be coming after you."

"That's the second time today I've been told to get out of town. I thought this was supposed to be warm and wonderful Florida."

"It's warm, but it's getting less and less wonderful. It's always been a sort of tacky, pirate kind of state. But in the last few years it's gone crazy. Everyone smells easy money. And I mean *everyone*. A week doesn't go by that some public character—sheriff, district attorney or judge—doesn't get indicted for being party to a drug ring. Smuggling's big. But land swindles are probably even bigger. Not the old land swindles, where real estate hacks sold swampland. The new swindles are smooth and efficient, and kept very hush-hush. It's always the same: Developers with big money buy off politicians. And then, arm in arm, they watch merrily while bulldozers and draglines convert what little wilderness the state has left into shiny new condominiums and trailer parks."

"I guess you have a right to sound bitter."

She smiled. "I guess I do—and not just because I'm native. I gave you my name, but I didn't give you my title. I'm *Dr.* Winnie Tiger, a state-employed biologist sent here three months ago to find out why the freshwater from all the canals in Cape Coral and Golden Gate is killing the fish in Florida Bay, and why the bald eagles are being slaughtered because certain developers have passed the word they'll pay a bounty for them. You can't cut down a tree with an eagle's nest in it, you see."

"Check me if I'm wrong, but it sounds like you already know why the fish and eagles are dying."

She nodded emphatically. "Of course I know. Most people do. But for a scientist to stop it, she has to build a very powerful case. Plenty of proof and cross proof. And it takes a long time. That's the way the developers and the politicians want it—land swindles, remember?"

Hawker rose to get more tea, cringing at the pain in his shoulder. "I didn't look under the bandage. You really sewed me up?"

The glow returned to her face. "I just grabbed a spare cat-gut suture and went at it. The shot of Demerol I gave you kept you woozy. I keep the stuff around to sew up 'coons and deer and stuff that catch the business end of cars on Tamiami Trail. I've got a bobcat healing out back, and his hide wasn't as tough as yours." She gave him a mock salute. "It's *Dr.* Winnie, remember. The closest people doctor is fifty miles by car, and you were losing so much blood I knew I had to do something quick. So I called Buck Hamilton—"

"Hamilton knows I'm in town?"

Buck Hamilton was the owner of the Tarpon Inn, Hawker's connection in Mahogany Key.

"He does. In fact, he raced right over to the Shop-and-Go and helped lug that big carcass of yours into your Monte Carlo. He followed us to my place and he lugged you into the bedroom, then lugged your clothes off you. That's a lot of lugging for a man Buck's age." She hesitated and added, "And you know he has that bad back—"

"Yeah, he told me last time I talked with him."

Hawker had never talked to Buck Hamilton. Jacob Montgomery Hayes had set up everything.

Winnie Tiger busied herself with her teaspoon. "He said he wants to see you as soon as you feel up to it."

Hawker rolled his shoulders, working some of the knots out. "I don't feel too bad now. I guess I'll grab my stuff and head over there—if you'll tell me where it is." Hawker had stood to go to the bedroom, but he stopped suddenly. He turned and gave Dr. Winnie Tiger a quizzical look. "I just realized something, woman."

"What's that—man?"

"In all this talking we've done, you never answered my original question: Who are those Colombians?"

Her eyebrows narrowed. "You ask an awful lot of questions for not being a cop."

"A businessman likes to know what he's getting into."

"Is that why this particular businessman carries an automatic pistol in his pocket?" She swung her head. "It's over on the stereo, by the way. I wanted to keep it handy."

Hawker retrieved the weapon and returned from the bedroom with his duffel. He leaned down and gave her a brotherly kiss on the forehead. "Thank you for everything, Doctor. You are truly one of the special ones."

As Hawker opened the front door of her little bayside cottage, she called out to him. "James!" He stopped and looked at her. She said, "I've only been here three months, so I'll let Buck explain the problems this town has." She tossed her hair back with a motion of her hand, and her brown eyes glistened. "But I will tell you this. If you stay after what happened this afternoon, they'll kill you. I know that. I know it's true. What's been going on here can't go on forever. Remember that, James. And I would hate to see this island's one brave man die for something that's going to change in time anyway."

James Hawker hesitated, then turned and walked alone into the Florida night.

They attacked when he got to his car.

He had no idea who they were. Hispanics. Two of them. The streetlight showed Hawker just enough to know they weren't part of the foursome he'd fought that afternoon.

One was a meaty, bowling-ball guy with long black greasy hair and hammers for fists.

The other was taller, thinner, with the high-pitched laugh of a psychopath.

Hawker had just opened the door of his Monte Carlo when two dark shapes materialized from the nearby trees. He saw them from the corner of his eye. He heard the metallic double click of a revolver being cocked and dove headlong toward the closest shape.

He hit the thin man hard, driving his head into his soft belly. The air went out of the man with a loud *whoosh* as they tumbled to the ground.

The lunatic had actually been laughing until he was hit. A strange, insane laugh that had made Hawker's hair stand.

With his head down and unable to see, Hawker pawed frantically with his right hand, trying to find the gun and wrestle it away.

Using the revolver as a club, the man with the psychopathic laugh pounded at the back of Hawker's neck. But they were too tightly locked for him to get any momentum behind the blows. Hawker finally got the man's left wrist in his right hand, snapped down brutally, and heard the damp *pop* as carpus bones broke.

The man released a muffled scream, and the gun flew away toward the shadows. Hawker cracked the man in the face with his elbow twice, hard. He did not scream again.

Hawker rolled away as the second man hit him. The man had to weigh well over two hundred pounds, and the impact sent the needles and bright colors of near-unconsciousness roaring through Hawker's head.

Somehow he got to his feet and stood face to face with the Hispanic. Hawker's left arm was worse than useless. The Hispanic threw a sidearm right. Hawker tried to duck, without success. The blow numbed his neck and knocked him to the ground.

As the Hispanic dove for him, Hawker got his knee up in time, burying it in the man's crotch. He moaned something in rapid Spanish. As he writhed in agony, Hawker fished the little Walther from his pocket and got shakily to his feet.

The psychopath was sitting up now. His nose had been crushed, and blood rivered down his face.

Hawker found his keys and swung open the trunk of the Monte Carlo. "Get in the car," he demanded in a hoarse whisper. "Move!"

"Not in the fucking trunk, man. We'll suffocate—"

"*MOVE!*"

The psychopath giggled as if he were delighted with the idea.

Hawker recovered the revolver, then drove north on the narrow road that lead to the Tamiami Trail. He pulled down the first dirt lane he found. It came to a dead end at the river.

Mosquitoes covered him in a veil as he opened the trunk.

"Get out. Keep it slow and easy. I'm going to ask you two some questions, and you're going to tell me more than I want to know or I'll give you each a third eye."

The heavy man got out stiffly, flexing his neck. Then the psychopath unfolded, a broad grin on his face. It took Hawker a moment to realize why he was grinning. It was like a bad dream, a slow-motion nightmare in grim shades of black and gray and mahogany: a perfect nightmare for Mahogany Key.

A stiletto had somehow materialized in the psychopath's right hand. He was on Hawker almost before he had a chance to react. He got the Walther up just in time and squeezed off a quick shot.

The psychopath's head exploded backward, spouting blood. He took three frantic steps and collapsed.

The big Hispanic crashed into Hawker a moment after he fired. Hawker's right hand found the man's windpipe, and he locked his grip on the throat, knowing that to release it was to die.

Hawker swung the Hispanic hard to the left, jerking away as hard as he could, feeling the tough, fibrous tube collapse in his hand.

The Hispanic clawed at his throat, his eyes bulging, making a strange grunting noise. He fell to the ground, kicking wildly. The sudden stillness was like a death certificate.

Hawker sagged against the car. "*Shit*," he whispered.

He had but one choice.

He opened the car door and switched on the headlights. The Chatham River was about twenty yards wide here. The water was tar black, moving in a slow flow. It looked deep.

Hawker noticed a set of fiery red eyes glowing from beneath the mangrove roots on the opposite bank. The eyes slowly submerged.

An alligator. And a big one.

Hawker found a chunk of rope near the spare tire in the trunk. He dragged the two corpses, one by one, to the edge of the river, then bound them tightly together.

He slid down the bank into the black river. The water was up to his neck, and cold. Hawker kept looking over his shoulder, as if it might help to see the 'gator before it hit him. He knew it was silly. If the 'gator wanted him, he wouldn't have a chance.

It took Hawker a little while to find the right spot. Finally, where the bank was undercut, the mangrove roots jutted out and then down, forming a tight cave.

Hawker pulled the corpses into the water with him, then used his own weight to force them under. Bubbles escaped from the dead lips as their mouths filled with water. Hawker jammed them into the underwater cave, tangling the rope deep in the roots and out of sight.

The rest would be up to the 'gator.

Hawker drove to the edge of the road, got out and broke the limb off a mangrove tree. He spent fifteen minutes obliterating the tire tracks of the Monte Carlo and his own footprints.

NINE

Before meeting Buck Hamilton at the Tarpon Inn, Hawker decided to have a quick drive around the town to gather his thoughts as well as familiarize himself with the island. He needed some time to settle down—and let his clothes dry.

There were two main streets. Bayside Drive snaked along the edge of the bay on the west side of the island. The more expensive houses sat overlooking the water, separated from the bay by the road. They were big stilt houses, mostly, with screened porches and tropical landscaping. Many of them looked abandoned, their windows dark.

From the street you could look far out onto the bay. A winter breeze threw a light chop across the water, rocking the boats at the public docks. Beyond the bay were the dark hedge shapes of mangrove islands. A half-moon held the bay in frozen light, turning distant waves to ice sculptures.

Beyond the mangroves, Hawker knew, was the open Gulf of Mexico. From there it was six hundred nautical miles to the Yucatán, or just over two hundred to Cuba.

At the north end of the island, Bayside Drive swung suddenly east. There was a small harbor here. A clustering of a dozen stilt houses outlined the harbor, which glistened with lights from the houses and big commercial boats.

Spanish rock 'n' roll and calypso music blared from the open windows of the houses, and men drank beer on the high porches.

At the northwesternmost point of the harbor was a squat wooden warehouse with a tin roof. There was a massive cement quay with a cranelike loading winch. Two lone silhouettes stood in the blue glare of antiburglar lights on the quay: guards.

Just beyond the warehouse was an opening in the pinelike casuarinas. Red and green ground lights marked both sides of the opening. The lights funneled into the distance.

It was a landing strip.

All too obviously, this was the Colombian stronghold. And they had chosen a good one. They could police it easily, on both the landward and seaward sides.

And from the air, too.

Hawker drove on.

Bayside Drive made a huge semicircle. At the north and south ends of the island, it was connected to Mahogany Key's second main street, Loggerhead Boulevard, which bisected the island. Loggerhead Boulevard was a pretty street with oak trees and greens and the old moon-globe streetlights. The houses here were neat and pleasant, shaded by trees.

Hawker drove past Winnie Tiger's place for the second time. It was a tiny little cottage of white clapboard and dark hurricane shutters. The yard, the little garden and the drive were all out-lined by rough coral rock.

It gave the place a safe and solitary look, like a haven.

As he idled past, he saw the Indian woman move across the scrim of lighted window: a dreamlike vision of face, and the outline of breasts and slim hips. He felt a deep sexual wanting tighten his stomach, and he realized it had been a long time since he had been with a woman.

And it would be longer yet. That he knew. He was on Mahogany Key on business. And he had a feeling it would turn into a very rough and brutal business before it was all over.

And he couldn't allow feelings for a woman to cloud his thinking or interfere with his work.

In Chicago he had become known as a loner, a tough cop who didn't like emotional attachments slowing him down.

And that was the way he wanted it, right?

Hawker's hand tightened on the steering wheel.

Right.

The Tarpon Inn had seen better days.

It was a little marina-type operation on the north lip of the island, where the dark water of the Chatham River emptied into the bay. Beyond the river was a hundred miles of mangrove swamp, sawgrass and cypress heads.

There were a half dozen outbuildings: a mechanic's shed, a concrete-block store that sold boating supplies and fishing tackle, a dry storage area for small boats, some ratty-looking storage dumps.

In the middle of the shell parking lot was a sign that advertised Gulf Gas and Cold Beer.

The sign was made of metal, and rust showed through the paint. The sign creaked in the wind.

There were a few cars and pickup trucks in the parking lot. Hawker swung in beside them.

The main building was built on stilts, half on land, half in the water. It looked like some Indiana barn that had lost its way.

The white paint was peeling, and an open porch reeled around the outside edge of the building, fifteen feet above the water. The sound of country-and-western music and the smell of fried food drifted outside into the night.

A lighted wooden sign on the tin roof of the building was in the shape of a giant jumping fish: Tarpon Inn, Restaurant and Lodging.

Hawker pulled open the door and went inside.

A few tables were filled with men in T-shirts and fishing hats, hunched in beery conversation. The bar's elegance was all out of proportion to the building that housed it. It was a massive curve of polished woods with brass rails. The walls were of pecky cypress. They were decorated with fishing rods crossed like sabers and mounted tarpon. The skins of the tarpon had turned to dark leather over the years.

As Hawker walked in, the room went immediately silent. The jukebox still played the whiskey voice of Waylon Jennings.

The men buried their eyes in their glasses, stealing looks at Hawker. Somehow they seemed to recognize him. Stories about his run-in with the Colombians must have spread quickly through the little island town.

The sudden fear that had filled the room evaporated. The men exchanged looks and seemed to nod in approval. A couple of them held their glasses out briefly in a gesture of greeting.

Hawker nodded back and went to the bar.

The bartender was a muscular, middle-size man in his late twenties. He had blond hair and a Burt Lancaster chin. His wire-rimmed glasses reflected the dim light of the bar.

Hawker took a stool. "Beer," he said. "Draft."

Hawker was surprised that the glass was frosted and the beer had been drawn with a proper head. "It's on the house," said the bartender when Hawker reached for his money. His speech was clipped with a hint of accent.

Hawker swallowed the beer. "Australian?"

"New Zealander," said the bartender.

"Why the free beer?"

"It's a courtesy we always extend to new owners." The bartender gave a crooked expression that must have been a smile. He held out his hand. "Graeme Mellor, Mr. Hawker. Word spreads fast on this island. You'll learn that." The crooked expression flashed across his face again. "You've only been here a day, and already you're one of Mahogany Key's leading citizens. Town hero, you bloody well are."

"Bloody well is right." Hawker chuckled. "The men in here all local?"

"Born and raised here. Fishermen, mostly. They run net boats or stone crab pullers. A couple of fishing guides, too. Old Harley Bates over there, the one in the khaki shirt with the Polaroids tied to his neck, has been written up in *Field and Stream* a couple of times. Knows more about fly fishing for tarpon than anyone in this part of Florida, supposedly. Works out of the marina here."

"Seems as if we don't have much female clientele."

Graeme Mellor winked and nodded. "Don't want any. Not in the bar, anyway. The Tarpon Inn began as a fishing and hunting club back in the 1920s. Men only. The rich and famous types heard about it and joined right up. Teddy Roosevelt, Clark Gable, Hemingway and some of his buddies, too. Hard to believe, looking at the place now. But back in those days the old Tarpon Inn was something. We've got their membership cards framed over in the lobby. The restaurant's open to ladies, but not the club bar. A few years ago some of them women's libbers came over in a caravan from Miami. Marched on the place, they did. Carried signs and sang songs, all for the television cameras."

"So what happened?"

The bartender smirked. "They made the mistake of coming in summer. You've never been here in the summer, Mr. Hawker. The mosquitoes and sand flies come at you in a cloud. After an hour those poor women only wanted to be liberated from the bugs. They hightailed it back to the big city, with those news people right after them." He laughed and gave Hawker a look of suspicion. "You wouldn't be meaning to open the place to women now, would you?"

Hawker was laughing himself. "If I changed anything, it would be to expand the men's part of the club."

Mellor nodded his approval as Hawker finished his beer. "Buck's over in the dining room waiting, Mr. Hawker."

"James. Mr. Hawker was my father."

"James it is, then. Anyway, Buck's looking forward to seeing you. No one comes to eat in the dining room much anymore, so the place is empty. You want me to have the cook fix you a nice dinner?"

Hawker realized that he hadn't eaten all day and that he was very hungry.

"What do you recommend?"

The bartender didn't hesitate. "Nice mess of stone crab claws, with a fillet of grouper on the side? Baked potato, if you want, but french fries would be quicker."

"Sour cream with the french fries, and Russian on the salad?"

Mellor flashed his funny smile again. "You'll be eatin' in twenty minutes. I'll stick a pitcher of beer in the freezer for you."

Buck Hamilton was a squat, bowlegged man with the shoulders and hands of a man three times his size. He wore a western plaid shirt with mother-of-pearl buttons. There was a garland of gray hair around the bald head, and bifocals gave him a professorial look. His jeans were belted tight around narrow hips, and there was nothing at all academic about his language.

"Goddamn," he bellowed, happy to meet Hawker, "I thought them spics had seen to it you leaked to death first day in town!"

Hawker smiled at the strength of the old man's handshake and took a seat across the table from him. Hamilton had a broad, Celtic face that was splotched by a lifetime spent in the tropic sun. His eyes were watery blue, and it was only in the eyes that Hawker could read the fear and worry the man had been suffering. Everything else about him suggested the likable bravado of a strong man who had spent his years in complete and total control of his own life.

Only his eyes told the truth: for once Buck Hamilton had lost control. And it frightened him.

"I want to thank you for helping Dr. Tiger, Buck. I came here to try and help you, and you end up saving my life."

Hamilton brushed away Hawker's thanks as if it were a fly. "Horse turds, boy! T'weren't nothing. You're the first one in this town to stand up to those mother dogs, and every man around just has to brag about what he'd of done if he'd of been in your shoes. It's upped my bar business fifty percent." He snorted in self-deprecation. "If I had a ball left between my legs, I'da hunted them down with a kill-gaff and made it so they had to say grace through their assholes." He thought for a moment, sobering. "In fact, if I'd had any balls at all, I'd of gotten some of the boys together and done it a year ago, when we first started having problems."

"Jacob Hayes told me a little bit about it. It didn't sound too good."

Buck Hamilton's head bowed as if under a weight. "How's old Jake doing, anyway? I wanted to cry when I heard about his boy. Only saw him once—about three years ago when Jake senior brought him down to catch his first tarpon. Fine-looking kid. Had a mind of his own, like his daddy." Hamilton took a little tin of snuff from his shirt pocket, jammed a ball of it inside his lip and spat into the brass spittoon near his chair, disgusted. "I'll tell you, James, this whole goddamn country has gone looney tunes. They let these crazy fuckers roam the streets, but they'll sure as hell throw an honest man's ass into jail if he kills a burglar trying to break into his house."

Hawker nodded and said nothing. Buck Hamilton was carrying a lot of bitterness and a lot of shame. Proud men don't like to ask for outside help. Hawker decided he would let Hamilton work into it his own way.

"And have you been to Miami lately?"

"Not since the early seventies."

Playing for the Tigers in the Florida Instructional League, Hawker had traveled most of the state.

"Shit, you wouldn't recognize Miami," Hamilton said. "Not since they brought in all them refugees from Mariel Harbor, Cuba, anyway."

"Buck," Hawker said softly. "You've got problems here. Let's talk about the Colombians."

Hamilton scratched his head and studied his feet. "Guess I have been going at it like a bird dog after a skunk, huh?" He looked at Hawker. "Fact is, I'm so ashamed of the way I and every man in this town has acted, it fairly makes my stomach roll. Don't even like to talk about it."

"The only difference between a coward and a brave man is the distance they'll let themselves be pushed. Maybe the men in your town have been pushed far enough," Hawker said.

At that moment the New Zealand bartender, Graeme Mellor, entered with Hawker's supper. The big yellow stone crab claws were piled high, and the fillet of grouper had to weigh two pounds. There was plenty of lime, sour cream, garlic toast and a bowl of drawn butter.

"That ought to keep you busy for a while," Mellor said with a grin.

"I hope so," said a suddenly subdued Buck Hamilton. "Mr. Hawker here is about to hear a very long and very sad story."

*　　*　　*

While Hamilton talked, Hawker did justice to the dinner.

He had had stone crab claws during his days as a catcher in the Tigers' organization, but these were even milder and richer than he remembered. He used nutcrackers to open them, dipped the pale meat in the butter, then ate them with the garlic toast. He washed it down with the iced beer, clearing the way for the lime-drenched grouper.

Hawker stopped long enough to ask a few questions during Hamilton's narrative. But mostly he listened. And ate.

The first Colombians had arrived a little over a year ago. There were four of them, all men. They said they wanted to go into commercial fishing. The townspeople helped them as they would have helped any newcomers. Then more Colombians arrived, buying boats and houses, flashing big money.

It wasn't long before things started to go sour.

There were a few separate incidents of Colombians ganging up on local fishermen in bar fights. Local people bristled, but it was generally accepted as inevitable when outsiders move into a historically hometown industry.

But then it got worse.

Men who defied the Colombians would go down to the docks one day to find their boats sabotaged. Nothing obvious: sand in the fuel tanks, or an accidental fire. If their defiance continued, the local fishermen would sail out to pull their stone crab traps, only to find the traps had been stolen.

After about four months the local fishermen had had enough. A group of them traveled to Tallahassee, Florida's capital, to complain. But their complaints were shrugged away as just those of more redneck racists who didn't like outsiders.

The Colombians, it seemed, had access to political power somewhere.

Upon the group's return, the fishermen had a town meeting and decided to clear the South Americans out on their own. But the fishermen were badly prepared, with almost no organization. The Colombians had already bought up most of their harbor stronghold by that time, and they were ready and waiting.

That night they beat the fishermen back savagely, almost killing a couple of them. And those few local men who remained standing were given a very clear message: The next time the townspeople tried to interfere in their business, the Colombians wouldn't stop at the men. They'd go for the women and children, too.

"I'll tell you, it took the starch out of 'most everybody," Buck Hamilton said. "We've had a couple of meetings since then, but all we did was bitch and bluster about what we ought to do. Nothing ever came of it. Them Colombians beat us bad, James. Men around here can't hardly look each other in the eye. They walk around with hangdog expressions like they got weights on their shoulders. And they're good men," Hamilton added fiercely. "It's just that we got out-toughed. It's embarrassing as hell, but it's true. The Colombians are just more ruthless and less vulnerable. And the worst thing is, the women and kids sense it, and they're scared worse than we are."

"The night you tried to fight them, who was your leader?"

Buck Hamilton sighed. "Hate to admit it, but I guess I was. We had the meeting here, and I led the boys down to Chatham

Harbor—that's where the Colombians are. Hell, I figured we'd just walk in there, kick ass and not bother with names. They got this huge mulatto called Simio—means 'gorilla' in Spanish, I guess. He's their ringleader's bodyguard. Well, Simio hit me a clip that knocked me out for a day and crossed my eyes for a week. I didn't get us equipped right, so our other boys didn't fare much better. Them Colombians are some kinda bad cattle, let me tell you."

Hawker remembered the name one of the Hispanics had used that afternoon. "Is their ringleader someone named Medelli?"

"Yeah, and he's a slick one, too. Shiny black hair, pencil-thin mustache and shit-pot full of gold chains on his neck and wrists. He lives out there in the Gulf on a yacht the size of a jetliner. Cruises up and down the coast, taking care of business. Funny thing is, the Coast Guard doesn't bother him. Medelli's got some pull somewhere."

"He never comes to Mahogany Key?"

"Oh, sure. Comes in to collect his drug money, I guess. He was here at the Tarpon Inn about a month ago. Brought that mulatto of his, Simio, with him. He swung a suitcase full of cash money on the bar and told me he was buying my place. I told him it wasn't for sale. He asked me how I'd like to end up as 'gator feed out in the 'Glades. I told them to get their asses out, and they left."

Hawker smiled. "After the beating you took, it's not the sort of thing a coward would do."

Hamilton looked sheepish, peering at Hawker through the bifocals. "I guess I didn't mention I was holding a double-barrel Winchester on them at the time, huh?"

The two men laughed, feeling comfortable in each other's company. The New Zealander brought Hawker key lime pie—pale yellow and delicate—and excellent espresso. They shifted the topic of conversation to more pleasant things.

Hawker asked questions about the operation of the inn and was assured Graeme Mellor could run the place blindfolded. As diplomatically as he could, he asked why the place had been allowed to fall into disrepair. Hamilton couldn't give him a good answer, but even before he finished, Hawker realized he had known the real reason all along: When people are stripped of their personal pride, they no longer take pride in their personal possessions.

It explained the creeping decay he had seen all over the island.

As Hawker stood to leave, he asked, "The night you fought the Colombians, did the other town leaders go with you?"

Hamilton wiped a massive hand across his face, thinking. "You mean like the mayor, or Ben Simps, chief of our one-man police force?"

Hawker shook his head. "No, not the figurehead leaders. You know the kind of men I mean—the kind of men people watch and listen to and admire, whether they admit it or not."

"I guess there's only one man in town who fits that description," Hamilton said after a moment. "Local boy I watched grow up. Boggs McKay. Hell of an athlete in high school, and went to Florida State on a football scholarship. Smart, too. No one really knows for sure, but some say he's got a masters degree in . . . something. He married up there, had kids. Made lots of money. But then something happened. Heard his kids got killed by some drunk driver, and then his marriage went on the rocks. Just showed up here about three years ago like he'd never left. Bought a boat and went to crabbing. Doesn't talk much; never talks about his past. But when Boggs McKay does talk, mister, people straighten right up and listen."

"Was Boggs with you that night?"

An amused smile settled on the face of Buck Hamilton. "Mr. Hawker, Boggs McKay doesn't follow *anybody anywhere*."

TEN

That night Hawker settled into his cottage. It was a garish rental cabin behind the main lodge, built of board and batten, painted flamingo pink.

There was a kitchenette, a sitting room with a black-and-white TV and a bedroom with a brass bed gone green from age. There were throw rugs on the linoleum, and the wall was rust streaked from the ancient air conditioner. With the windows open, you could hear the tidal rush and an occasional guttural heron cry from the Chatham River outside.

Hawker stripped off his clothes and went to the mirror.

The Colombian's knife had dug a six-inch furrow in his shoulder. Dr. Winnie Tiger's stitches were like black teeth. The wound intersected an older scar: in December of 1975 he had gotten stabbed trying to break up a bar fight on Chicago's South Side.

He flexed the shoulder and stretched the muscles until sweat beaded on his forehead.

His nose had clogged with blood again. He blew it clean, then stopped the bleeding with a styptic pencil and nasal spray.

When he could breath again, Hawker showered. He turned the water as hot as he could stand it, then as cold as it got. He pulled on thick cotton sweat pants and a soft black rugby jersey, then set about opening the crates Jacob Montgomery Hayes had shipped down from Chicago for him.

He placed the 128K RAM computer on the little desk near the telephone, then mounted the video screen atop it. He patched in the telephone modem and the second disk drive, then checked it all to make sure it worked.

It did.

There were three crates of weaponry. He opened only one. From it he took a 9-millimeter Ingram MAC11 submachine gun. It wasn't much bigger or heavier than a standard .45 automatic pistol. The silencer was longer than the weapon itself, and Hawker threaded it on. He filled the thirty-two-round clip, then armed the weapon before sliding it under his bed.

From the crate he produced a Colt Commander .45 automatic. It wasn't the sort of weapon he could carry in his pants pockets, but it was among his favorite heavy-shooting handguns. He had had the Commander customized by Devel Corporation in Cleveland, master gunsmiths. They had chopped it, making it more compact, and added a Swenson speed safety. There was a low-mounted Bo-Mar rear sight and a bright yellow insert on the front ramp sight. Among other things, the Devel people had customized it with an electroless nickel finish, giving the pistol a satin silver appearance that made it look even more lethal.

He placed the Colt Commander under his pillow.

In another crate Hawker found the Marconi-Elliott Avionicbuilt alarm system. It was an improved version of the old Tobias Seismic system.

He decided six of the little radio-operated seismic plates would be sufficient and carried them outside. The night had turned blustery, with cloud scud speeding past the winter moon. Streetlights rattled in the wind. Hawker found a shovel in one of the sheds and buried the seismic plates in the sandy soil one by one. He positioned them in a fifty-meter circle around his cabin and along the back lane that exited from his cottage and the Tarpon Inn onto Bayside Drive. To test them he turned the Monte Carlo's radio on low and went inside.

The main unit was housed in an aluminum briefcase. Hawker snapped it open and scanned the rows of knobs and toggle switches. There was a general audio alarm, guarding all four channels. The alarm was on: an irritating whine. Hawker flipped it off. A needle bounced in visual alarm on the channel tuned to the area around the drive. Hawker placed the earphones on his head. He could hear the music plainly—and the nearest seismic radio plate was twenty yards from the rental car.

Satisfied, he went outside and turned off the radio, then returned the unit to general four-channel alarm guard.

Hawker turned his attention to the computer. On a piece of paper he scribbled the names he wanted to check: Chief Ben Simps, Boggs McKay, Medelli, Pedro Cartagena, Graeme Mellor and Dr. Winnie Tiger. He didn't have high hopes of getting much information on the Colombians, but he could try. He had a telephone, and information operators—and data banks—around the world never slept.

As he booted the machine with his outlaw RUSTLED software, something suddenly touched one of his own memory electrodes:

"Perhaps one day I will find you alone, and I will show you what a coward Pedro Cartagena is . . ."

The words the Colombian had used to threaten Winnie.

Quickly Hawker pulled on his running shoes and found four more of the seismic plates. They would transmit over a mile, and her cottage was less than five blocks away.

Outside, he relocated the shovel. He hoped she was asleep and wouldn't hear him digging in her yard.

It was two A.M. by the ghostly glow of his submariner watch.

Down the bay he could see lights at Chatham Harbor. Maybe the Colombians were bringing in another load.

Hawker had hidden his anger from Buck Hamilton and the rest. Now it all came rushing up. James Hawker's eyes narrowed to slits as he studied the distant harbor.

"Try me again, you bastards," he whispered in the night. *"Try me now that I'm ready. Please."*

ELEVEN

Hawker fell easily into the role of owner of the Tarpon Inn.

He even enjoyed it.

He had had two careers in his life, and this was the first that didn't demand he wear a uniform. Graeme Mellor slowly introduced him to the day-by-day operation of the lodge and was soon insisting that Hawker take control.

With little hesitation Hawker did just that. As far as Mellor and the rest were concerned, Hawker really was the new owner.

One of the hardest things was getting Buck Hamilton to leave town. Hawker finally had to take him aside and insist on it, reasoning that no one would believe the cover story if Buck hung around and persisted in giving orders to the staff.

A call from Jacob Montgomery Hayes inviting Buck to a duck hunt didn't hurt. Even so, Hamilton left grudgingly, vowing to return in time to help Hawker "kick a little Colombian ass!"

Everyone was sorry to see him go, including Hawker.

The lodge had three full-time staff members: Mellor, who

tended bar and took care of the ordering; Sandy Rand, a buxom, good-natured blond waitress who also cleaned rooms; and Logan, a huge bearded Vietnam vet who was known both for his temper and his poet's touch in the kitchen. Of the three, Logan was the hardest to get to know. But Hawker made it clear that of the many problems the Tarpon Inn had, bad cooking was not one of them. Soon Logan was offering morning pleasantries, even smiling.

And the Tarpon Inn *did* have problems. Over the past year Buck Hamilton had allowed the place to go to hell. As Hawker well knew, it was a common problem. Discontent had spread through the community like an epidemic. And the epidemic was fear. Fear infested the island, and every business suffered. Mahogany Key was like a microcosm of Jacob Montgomery Hayes's American parable: Now was the village's time of chaos. In time—a very short time—the town would heave a final gasp and die.

Hawker and Mellor often talked about it after the bar had closed, sitting over cold beer.

Hamilton's first mistake had been to concession out the marina part of the operation. The couple running the marina were a man and woman who hadn't matured out of their late-sixties hippiehood. They wore their hair in ponytails, and they were rude and impatient with customers. Business hours at the marina varied with the amount of dope they had smoked the night before.

Hawker tried talking to them, but they treated him with the same contempt their customers suffered.

It was a mistake they wouldn't make again.

Hawker made a phone call and, with Buck Hamilton's bless-ings, gave the two their walking papers. He did some scout-ing around and found a third-generation Mahogany Key man whose boat had been sabotaged by the Colombians. He had a wife and four sons, and only the little bit of pride he had left kept him from applying for welfare.

Hawker invited him to the marina, showed him around and offered him the place on a straight percentage basis. There would also be a percentage bonus for any net volume that exceeded profits of the previous year. He could hire two of his sons to work around the marina, and they would all be covered under a new co-op workers' compensation and hospitalization plan Mellor had already arranged. Benefits would be paid for from the marina's gross.

The man became misty eyed as he accepted Hawker's offer, vowing to give Tarpon Inn the best damn marina south of Sanibel.

To be sure he had the customer flow to do it, Hawker enlisted the ready aid of Dr. Winnie Tiger. He had seen Winnie just about every day since his arrival. The first week she had insisted on checking his stitches. The second week he had insisted on accompanying her on field studies. He had an ulterior motive in this, since it also gave him a chance to learn the lay of the land; it was knowledge he might need if he had to lead an assault team through back country.

He had Winnie, who was a competent photographer, get some shots of the marina fishing guide, Harley Bates, catching tarpon. Hawker picked the best of the photos, and he and Win-nie pasted up an advertising layout on what Tarpon Inn had to offer. The rest of the photos were sent to major sporting magazines around the country, asking editors if they were willing to trade expensive advertising space for a few days' free fishing on Mahogany Key.

Many were.

Hawker knew he was getting the lodge—and the town—going in the proper direction. But he also knew it wasn't enough. So he made a long-distance call to Jacob Montgomery Hayes.

"Jacob, I need two hundred thousand dollars."

Hayes didn't hesitate. "As I said, I'm happy to give you whatever you need—"

"It's not a gift I want. It's a loan."

Hawker explained about the improvements he wanted to make. "But it can't be a gift, Jacob. I'll sign the note—not that I'm good for it. The people in this town will pay you back, though, once their dignity's returned to them. And getting these people working at something again will be a step in the right direction. A gift of money will just make them bitter in the long run. There's no pride in accepting handouts."

So Hawker got his money the next day by wire. Graeme Mellor knew the Tarpon Inn a lot better than Hawker, so it was he who designed improvement plans. But it was Hawker who insisted that they draw completely on the resources of the community for labor and supplies. Mahogany Key's small hardware store and its trucking business had both all but closed as a result of the disastrous year the fishermen were having. Hawker had meetings with the owners of both and awarded each big orders, paying cash.

Hawker knew that in each community, there are men and women who, whatever their occupations may be, are craftsmen with wood or design or landscaping. He tracked these people down, employing just as many of the villagers as he could. Most were fishermen. All were more than ready to work at something constructive.

Their job was to return to the Tarpon Inn Lodge the splendor it had known when it was the hangout of Teddy Roosevelt, Clark Gable, Hemingway and the rest.

As he hired each individual, Hawker demanded only a full day's work for a full day's pay. It wasn't long before he realized he didn't have to ask. Enthusiasm for the project grew quickly. Workers began at first light and refused to quit until the streetlights came on. Everything was being renovated: the grounds, the foundations, the interior and exterior, even the docks.

Word spread around the island. And Hawker saw the change come over the people—people he was getting to know and who seemed to return his respect and friendship. As they watched the lodge being transformed from a rambling old hulk into a showplace, the decay of their own homes suddenly seemed intolerable.

Pride is a contagious thing.

Lawns were mowed, gutters were repaired and buildings were painted. It didn't happen all at once. But it was happening.

More important, as the people began to take pride in their town, they regained some of their self-esteem.

People hazarded smiles again. They waved at each other on the downtown streets again.

But there was still a shadow. And James Hawker knew that before Mahogany Key could be a healthy, thriving village again, that shadow had to be removed.

The reprisal he expected from his fight with the Colombians had yet to come. And he knew why. Using one of the marina's little rowboats, he had been making nightly trips to Chatham Harbor, the Colombian stronghold. Spying on them was risky business. Once he had almost been spotted hiding in the mangroves in the little skiff when one of the guards unexpectedly flicked on a searchlight.

Two other times he had found himself within twenty meters of someone lurking in the mangrove swamps. The first time he thought it was one of the Colombian guards. The second time, though, Hawker realized the guy was as anxious to avoid detection as he was.

Someone else, it seemed, was keeping the Colombians under surveillance. It was just another mystery in this increasingly complex puzzle.

The investigating he had done through his computer had confused him as much as it had helped him. He had tried data banks in Bogotá and found only that Pedro Cartagena—the man he had fought his first day in town—was a member of a Central American ultra left-wing guerrilla army known as the Tigre squad.

Hawker had heard of that band of lunatics before, and it sent off a gang of alarms in his head. Finally he remembered: the Guatemalan who had murdered young Jake Hayes had been a member of the same organization.

But Bogotá didn't have a file on Medelli—not one that could be unlocked, anyway.

On a hunch he tried the data banks in Washington. There he got a brief file on both Medelli and his mulatto bodyguard,

Simio. Medelli was a jet-set Colombian playboy who had been granted a diplomatic position in the United States in return for political favors. Simio had been involved in a number of bar fights in Washington, D.C., almost killing one man. Because of diplomatic immunity, he had never even been arrested.

Both of them were aides to an upper-echelon South American diplomat. Hawker didn't recognize the name. But if he had been the interpreter on the phone the night Jake Hayes was murdered, he would have.

The diplomat's name was Guillermo.

Somehow it all fit together.

Hawker didn't know how.

But he did find out why the South Americans had not come after him right away. They had been unloading, warehousing and transporting a massive drug shipment. Their men had been working almost around the clock.

But the work wouldn't last forever. Soon their ringleader, Medelli, would come cruising in to collect his dirty money—and there would be a confrontation.

Hawker still had much to do, and not much time.

He sensed war in the wind.

And that war was all too soon in coming.

TWELVE

It began on a Friday night the second week in January, a night of cold bright stars and a south wind that smelled of open sea and Cuba.

The noise was a high-pitched whine, like bees.

Hawker incorporated the noise into his dream. In the dream he had rounded the stone corner of the barn in his birthplace of Dun Dealgan, on the moonscape coast of northeastern Ireland.

It was the dream in which his mother and three older sisters are destroyed by the bomb. The dream in which there is a yellow shock of heat and light, and the terrible ringing in a tiny boy's ears.

His ears.

It was the dream in which the young Irish father runs screaming toward the smoking cottage, crying vengeance on heaven and hell, and Ulster's Orange Order.

James Hawker had never seen his father cry before that day.

He never saw his father cry after that day.

But this time the dream was different. There was the flash

of yellow as the bomb exploded, and the *whack* and *thump* as pieces of the stone cottage fell to earth. But there was no ringing in the little boy's ears.

There was, instead, the strange whining.

Like bees . . .

Hawker jolted upright in bed, rolling to the floor. Sweat coated his face, and adrenaline raced through him. Beside him on the table, the seismic intruder alarm droned out a general alert.

Calmer now, Hawker found the little Ingram submachine gun under the bed and moved to the window. He had not pulled out the sliding stock, and the weapon was like a handgun in his big fist. The silencer made it bow heavy.

It was a warm night, and he peered through the screen. It was a night without moon. Light from the street lamps filtered through the trees. The hood of his Monte Carlo was open, and a man was hunched over the engine. Another man stood guard.

Hawker wondered if they were Colombians or if they were just two local kids trying to steal a battery. He decided to watch for a time before doing anything.

The men finished their work. They closed the hood of the car and did a Keystone Cops pantomime, tiptoeing away. They carried no battery.

Hawker decided to follow. He pulled on jeans, soft-soled shoes and a black sweater of oiled wool. The sweater was rough against his skin. He pulled his pants up and strapped a Gerber Mark II attack knife in an ankle sheath to his leg. He grabbed the Ingram, found the proper toggle channel on the seismic intruder alarm and flicked it off.

The whine of the general alarm continued.

He gave the aluminum case a rap, thinking it had jammed. Then he stopped, frozen in slow realization. He fumbled for the desk light and switched it on. The visual indicators on the alarm unit were mounted in plastic disks, like the volume meters on some stereo systems.

One needle flapped madly in its case. It was the channel frequencied to the transmitters at Winnie Tiger's cottage.

Cursing his stupidity, Hawker charged out the screen door into the darkness. He didn't slow at his car. The men he had seen weren't teenagers looking for spare parts. He knew that now. The car had been booby-trapped.

It was revenge night for the Colombians. The thought of how they might take their revenge on Winnie Tiger sickened him.

He sprinted down Bayside Drive, gravel grinding beneath his shoes. There was a hedge and a chain-link fence. He hurdled them both, running hard through the shadows.

In the distance he could see lights on at her cottage.

Hawker pounded across the boulevard, shoulders low, thighs driving.

There were dim shapes in the yard. A man was bent over the figure of a woman. The woman lay still as death. A streetlight swung in the wind, painting the ground with light. Every two strides the light swung, and he could see the woman's face. It was coated in a black mask, like tar. Or blood. Something protruded from the face. Hawker wondered grimly how anyone could put a knife in those haunting, earthen eyes.

"*You—freeze!*" Hawker heard a strange, hoarse yell. It was a moment before he realized the words were his own. He held the

Ingram ready, hoping the man would make a move so he could cut him in two.

"Mr. Hawker? James?" The man was huge, with a beard. He moved out of the shadows. Hawker recognized the face and the voice. It was the chef from the Tarpon Inn.

"Logan! Is she dead? What the hell are you doing here?"

The man made a helpless motion, like a bear. "It's like you told us—that neighborhood-watch-program thing. Every night one of us—Graeme or Sandy or me—would walk past Dr. Tiger's house after we got off work from the lodge. You know, to make sure everything was okay." Logan's voice thickened. Even the Vietnam vet had been shaken by the sight on the ground. He made the helpless motion again. "Tonight I got here too late."

The woman lay on the ground, her hands clawed out as if to stop a fall.

But there was no stopping this fall.

The knife had been plunged in to the hilt. The waitress uniform had been ripped away. The material was black splotched from the wound. Her breasts were heavy and pale, flattened against her rib cage by their own weight. Her dress had been pulled over meaty thighs, the legs crossed in final defiance.

It took Hawker a long, confused moment before he realized what he was seeing.

"Christ," he whispered. "This isn't Winnie. It's Sandy."

Sandy Rand had been the waitress at the Tarpon Inn. She was a garrulous blonde who chewed gum, read scandal sheets, flirted scandalously and did the work of three people. Hawker had liked her.

"Logan—where's Winnie?"

The huge man seemed not to hear. He stood over the corpse, head bowed, arms long and slack. "It was my night to take the watch," he recited softly. "But she said, 'Logan, honey, you got more work to do, so I'll just go by that pretty Indian girl's place.' She told me to come by her apartment later. She . . . she was the only one I ever told how I didn't like being alone since . . . since Nam, and she would hold me sometimes—"

"Logan!"

"And then I go and let this happen to her . . ."

Hawker took the man by the shoulders and shook him softly. "Logan, listen to me! It's not your fault. Do you hear? Where's Winnie? Do they still have Winnie?"

A screen door slammed. "No. They don't have Winnie. Winnie was safe and sound inside. She was listening to pretty music on the stereo while this poor girl was fighting for her life," Dr. Winnie Tiger said as she came across the lawn, arms folded across her white nightgown.

The orange eye of a cigarette glowed in her right hand. Hawker remembered her telling him she loathed smoking. She took an uncomfortable drag from the cigarette and threw it to the ground.

He expected her to race to his arms. Or collapse into tears. She did neither. Her mahogany face was like an Aztec mask. She reached out and took his hand in hers, squeezing it. "I called Chief Simps," she said.

"You're sure you're okay?"

She nodded. She noticed that little submachine gun for the first time. "How did you know, Hawker? I tried to call, but there was no answer."

Hawker asked, "Who did it, Winnie? Did you get a look?"

91

"Too close of a look. You didn't see him?"

His expression was puzzled.

She nodded toward the chef. "Logan didn't show you the other corpse? He didn't show you Sandy Rand's killer?"

"Other corpse?"

"On the other side of the rock wall. Near the road. I'd rather not see it twice."

"Logan killed him?"

"He says not. You decide for yourself. He's in shock, you know. Keep an eye on him. He was in love with Sandy, and she had a thing for him." For the first time she seemed near tears. "I feel so . . . so damn bad about it all, Hawk. She must have seen the son of a bitch snooping outside my cottage, and maybe questioned him or something. She—she was trying to protect me."

Hawker held her close for a moment, then disentangled himself. Logan still stood over the body of Sandy Rand, his head bowed reverently. He had taken off his jacket and covered her. Hawker walked past him and stopped at the rock wall.

A siren wailed in the distance.

The streetlight still rocked in the wind. Palm fronds rattled.

Pedro Cartagena lay on his back in the damp grass. His face was frozen in a grotesque snarl, the Fu Manchu mustache spread across his face, teeth bared. His arms were locked in close to his body, fingers splayed toward his shoulders, as if fighting the device that had killed him.

He had not died easily. Or prettily.

A black line, as clean—but not as deep—as a razor's slice encircled his neck. The Colombian's eyes bulged.

He had been garroted. Strangled with a wire.

Three blocks away a police car skidded through the turn, blue light pulsing.

Hawker hurried. With his foot he turned the dead man on his side. There was a gurgling noise and a sudden fecal stench mixed with the sheared-metal stink of blood. Hawker found the billfold and slid it into his own pocket.

He felt someone beside him. It was Winnie. She had watched him, and her face was filled with worry and suspicion.

"Who are you, James Hawker?" She seemed to be asking some person beyond his own eyes. "I want to know who you are. Why won't you trust me?"

Hawker turned away and took the Gerber Mark II from the ankle sheath. He wiped the blade and black handle clean and forced the dead man's right fist closed around it.

The police car skidded to a halt in the drive. The dome light blinked on as a squat, heavyset man got out.

Hawker went to Logan and squeezed his arm, hard. "I've got to make this quick, Logan. Listen good. I don't care if you killed that bastard or not. In fact, I hope you did—"

"I didn't kill him."

"*I don't care, understand?* But they're going to figure you did it. And if you decide you want to admit it, remember: He came at you with a knife. Not the knife that killed Sandy. Another knife, a knife like a dagger."

"I didn't see any other knife."

"It's in his right hand. I put it there."

The huge head turned as if on a turret. The shock-glazed eyes cleared momentarily. He nodded his understanding. "Thanks, James. But I didn't kill him."

A baritone voice with a hint of drawl came from over Hawker's shoulder. "Well, somebody sure as hell has been doing some killing around here. You boys wouldn't be trying to put together some bullshit story for me, now, would you?"

Chief Ben Simps, head of Mahogany Key's one-man police force, came across the lawn adjusting his gun belt. He was a wide, military-looking man carrying too much fat. The leather holster creaked as he walked.

Hawker had yet to meet him. He had hoped to get together, individually, with both Simps and Boggs McKay when he and the townspeople were ready to strike the Colombians.

He had hoped that would be in about another month.

Now he knew it would be sooner. Much sooner.

"The killer is dead, Chief Simps. He's over by the rock wall."

Simps looked at him sharply. "Are you an eyewitness?"

"No."

"Did you kill the man who you say is the killer?"

"No."

"Then who appointed you spokesman? When I want something out of you, Mr.—"

"Hawker. James Hawker. I bought the Tarpon Inn from Buck Hamilton."

"When I want something out of you, Mr. Hawker, I'll ask. Until then, just keep quiet, hear?"

"Spare me the Marshal Dillion bit, Simps," Hawker said softly. "I know a bit too much about you to let it slide."

The cop whirled, as if he welcomed the confrontation. But then he caught the look in Hawker's eyes. It stopped him. He backed up a step, nervous under Hawker's gaze. He noticed the weapon in Hawker's hands and seemed thankful for the chance to be on the offensive again.

"Where in the hell did you get that?"

Hawker toyed with the idea of saying he had found it on the lawn. He had been damn stupid to bring the Ingram submachine gun.

"It's mine," Hawker said. "With all the killing going on in this peaceful little town, I thought it was appropriate."

Simps held out his hand. "I'll take it. Uncle Sam has a thing about private citizens carrying automatic weapons."

Hawker made no effort to give him the Ingram. "That's right. I guess that's why they make people in my occupation carry them."

Hawker had no permit. But he had given Simps the proper impression. He wanted him to think he was a federal cop. Hawker watched his reaction closely. Ben Simps didn't seem the kind of man to be intimidated easily. But he was intimidated now.

The meaty face swung around, checking to make sure the other two couldn't hear them. Simps said, "What did you mean, you know too much about me?"

Hawker strung together the list of facts he had gotten from his computer check on Ben Simps. It was an impressive list. Simps had once been a cop in Miami, a crooked cop who knew how to play the game. He had won some commendations. Hawker named the commendations. Unexpectedly, Simps had resigned from the force. Hawker guessed at the reason why, and he could see in Simps's face that he was right.

"You got caught taking payoff money, Simps. Until then your record had been pretty clean—but only because they'd never caught you before, never caught you shaking down whores and bar owners and pimps. So they gave you a choice: Quit the force, or hang around and be indicted. So you stuck your tail between your legs and ran—ran right here to Mahogany Key."

"And I've been trying to do a good job," Simps said quickly. "But Christ, this place has gone crazy in the last year. You know where the county seat is? Key West! The damn county seat is a hundred miles by water or two hundred miles by car, so I'm stuck out here in the damn 'Glades without any help—"

"The Colombians are helping you, aren't they? The people in this town aren't dumb. You drive a big new car and own a big new houseboat. They can put two and two together. So can we, Simps. Maybe some friends of mine at the IRS should get down here and do a net-worth investigation—"

"Shit, not that, Hawker—or whoever you are." Simps had grabbed his arm. He was pleading. "Look, they forced me. They threatened me and my wife. I'll do anything. I'll turn state's evidence. You just name it, and I'll do it."

Hawker pulled away from him. "You've got a murder to investigate, Chief Simps. Hadn't you better get started? Or do you just sort of turn your head when one of your Colombian friends kills an innocent woman?"

"Anything," Simps whispered feverishly. "I'll do anything. Christ, I've got grandkids. Don't send me to jail."

"That woman with the knife in her eye had more courage in her little finger than a dozen of your kind, Simps," Hawker said coldly. The hook was in, and Hawker set it. "Unfortunately, I'm going to be needing you. I'll tell you when, where and what. Until then, investigate your murder."

Simps turned away, grateful. His face was shiny with sweat. But then his cop instincts made him look at Hawker again. "You didn't show me any identification. How do I know you're who you say you are?"

"I don't remember telling you I was anything but owner of the Tarpon Inn." There was a metallic edge to Hawker's voice. "And that's the way it's going to stay. Personally I'd like to see you trucked off with the others when we finally clean this place out. It's up to you."

"I'll help," Chief Ben Simps said quickly. "I'll help and I won't ask any more questions."

Simps adjusted his gun belt. He hurried away toward the corpse.

THIRTEEN

"Did you learn anything about explosives in the Marines?"

Hawker and Logan walked beneath trees down the boulevard toward the Tarpon Inn.

It was 3 A.M.

"I was a cook."

Hawker knew he was lying. His computer check had told him Logan had been a Marine sergeant, twice winner of the Bronze Star. On his last tour in Nam, he had been placed with a squad of Navy SEALS. He was a demolitions expert. From the gaps in his record, Hawker guessed he had also done some work for I-Corps, military intelligence. Hawker now began to suspect he worked for the FBI—or the CIA.

Someone else had been monitoring the activities of the South Americans. Hawker wondered if it was Logan.

"What kind of cook?"

"A very good one."

"And you didn't kill the Colombian?"

Logan gave him a warning look. He had already answered

his share of questions. Chief Ben Simps had done a professional and complete preliminary investigation, probably to impress Hawker. Through an arrangement with Monroe County, Mahogany Key's county, Collier County had sent a coroner's wagon for the bodies. Simps had questioned Winnie Tiger and Logan individually. He had asked them the same things over and over.

Their answers were always the same. Winnie had been in bed, listening to the stereo. She had had no idea what had happened until Logan pounded on the door. Logan said he had been on the way to Sandy Rand's apartment when he heard a scream. He couldn't tell if it was a man screaming or a woman. Both Sandy and the Colombian were dead when he got there.

"So who killed the Colombian?"

Logan's eyes burrowed into Hawker's. "Didn't you? The way you planted the knife was pretty slick. You're no amateur, Hawker. I figure you're just trying to protect your cover—and I don't even want to guess why. But you're more than just the new owner of the Tarpon Inn."

"And you were more than just a cook in the Marines."

"That's right. I was a *very good* cook in the Marines. So let's drop it, huh? I don't know who killed that greasy bastard, but I'd like to thank him."

"And I don't suppose you've been slipping out at night, watching the Colombians from the mangroves in Chatham Harbor?"

Logan stopped and jammed his fists on his hips. "Look, Hawker, I like you. And I appreciate what you're trying to do for the people in this town. So let's cut the bullshit, huh? I don't want any part of your cops-and-robbers games. I've had a stomach full of that crap. I just want to cook, okay? Let's leave it at that. I'm just a cook."

"Not tonight, you're not," Hawker said softly. "Tonight you're more than a cook."

"And just what in the hell do you mean by that—"

"I need your help, that's what I mean. I'll show you."

Hawker was surprised to see lights on in the Tarpon Inn bar. Graeme Mellor was still up. He wondered if someone had called and told him about the murder of Sandy Rand.

He led Logan down the drive to his flamingo-pink cottage. Birds were making their first tentative morning sounds. They rattled in the dark trees.

Hawker stopped at the Monte Carlo. "I saw two Colombians messing with my car tonight. They had the hood up."

Logan's knees cracked and popped as he squatted at the grille. He looked at it without touching it. "You have a flashlight?" Hawker went into his cottage and produced a flashlight.

"Did they close the hood like they were trying to be particularly careful?"

"Quiet. But not that careful."

"Do you have a wife and kids—people who need you around?" Logan's hand was under the grille, looking for the hood latch.

Hawker smiled. "No."

"Good." Logan swung the hood open. Both men exhaled loudly. They had been holding their breath.

"It's a pretty simple device," said Logan.

In the white beam of the flashlight, Hawker could see two

sticks of dynamite joined by electrician's tape. Two lengths of copper wire ran to something in the engine.

"It's an ignition bomb," Logan continued. "The wire runs to the solenoid, then back to that blasting cap taped to the dynamite. Starting the car both provides the current and completes the circuit."

"I thought you were a cook."

"In the Marines they blew up bad cooks. I had to learn about these things."

"Boom," whispered Hawker.

"*Ka*-boom," Logan said. "Two sticks of dynamite, remember? You want me to take it off?"

"Unless you're in the market for a Monte Carlo. I'll sell it right now. Cheap."

"Get some wire cutters."

"I'll get the wire cutters if you'll help me when you're done. I don't like people planting bombs in my car."

"Oh? You never struck me as the fussy sort."

"The car has sentimental value. I've leased it for almost two months."

Hawker turned to go into his cottage. Logan called after him, "Thanks for killing that Colombian, Hawker."

"Thank *you* for killing the Colombian, Logan," Hawker said over his shoulder.

Hawker and Logan removed the ignition bomb. Hawker wrapped it in canvas, and the two of them headed for the airstrip.

It was 4:13 A.M.

They could see two guards in the fluorescent glare of the Chatham Harbor warehouse. One sat with his legs over the dock. The other leaned on his rifle, bored.

Moored at the deep-water quay was an oceangoing yacht. It must have been a hundred feet long. It had a white hull with blue superstructure. There were Boston Whalers on davits, bow and stern, covered with canvas.

The stern of the vessel read: *Demonio Del Mar, Bogotá.*

Hawker had never seen the yacht before. Buck Hamilton had described it to him. It made Hawker wonder why the Colombians had chosen this as their night for revenge. Why would they risk a retaliatory strike—not to mention trouble with the law—while Medelli, their leader, was in town? It didn't make any sense. Hawker wondered if it had all been a personal vendetta carried out by Pedro Cartagena and a few of his friends.

But Medelli wouldn't like one of his men being killed. And he would like even less what Hawker and Logan were about to do.

"Do you know the guy who owns that boat?"

Logan shook his head. "Can't say I've had the pleasure."

"Let's give him a warm welcome."

"Did he have anything to do with killing Sandy?"

"He had a lot to do with it—but indirectly."

"Let's make it *real* warm."

They skirted the harbor, staying low. Hawker led the way. The field trips with Dr. Winnie Tiger had been a big help. They waded across a shallow creek and weaved their way through underbrush. Hawker threw himself to the ground belly first. The airstrip arrowed away before them. Newly mown, it smelled of grass.

The red and green landing lights were off, and January stars glimmered above the field.

There was only one plane: a three-engine Trislander. It rested on the far side of the airstrip. It looked big enough to carry fourteen or fifteen people.

There were two more guards near the plane. They carried long guns: automatics.

They paced opposite sides of the runway, their weapons slung over their shoulders.

"Shit," whispered Logan. "Looks like we're not going to be able to plant our little surprise."

"Maybe you ought to look the other way," Hawker whispered back.

"What's that supposed to mean?"

"It means if we somehow get arrested, you'd be in better shape if you could honestly tell them you don't know a damn thing about what I'm about to do."

Hawker disappeared through the trees before Logan had a chance to reply.

He made his way parallel to the runway, moving silently through the palmetto cover. The one thing he had going in his favor was that the guards patrolled in opposite directions rather than marching side by side.

As the guard closest to him walked east, Hawker went west.

At the base of the runway was a decrepit-looking tank truck. They probably used it for fuel. Hawker waited until the guard was at the farthest point from him, then sprinted to the cover of the truck.

He'd left his Gerber with the corpse, so he'd have to improvise. He figured he could club the guard closest to him, then rush the other before he had a chance to react.

As the first guard drew near, Hawker stepped out and cracked the man's head open with the Ingram. The blow would have knocked most men unconscious. But the guard wasn't most men. He screamed out a warning before Hawker kicked his mouth closed.

The clatter of automatic-weapons fire sounded from across the field. The dirt near Hawker erupted in a series of explosions. Hawker dove, rolled and came up shooting. The silencer made the Ingram sound like a series of soft, thudding drumbeats.

Thirty yards away the guard jolted three feet into the air before landing back first on the asphalt runway.

Hawker waved Logan in.

Logan was surprisingly calm. "Not bad," he said. "You shoot pretty good."

"Never mind about that. Get to work on the plane."

"You really think they're going to try to fly that thing after they've found their two guards dead?"

"By the time I get done, they will. I'm going to make it look like they got in a fight and killed each other. They're a damn violent bunch, and they don't always save aggression for enemies."

"Good trick."

"Spend time as a Chicago cop and you learn a lot of good tricks. But my tricks aren't going to help us unless you get your ass in gear."

When Hawker was done staging the corpses, he maintained battle-ready, the Ingram on his hip, while the big Vietnam vet worked. It didn't take Logan long.

Even so, it was nearly dawn before they headed back.

They moved quietly through the thickets of Brazilian pepper and mangrove that edged both sides of the airstrip. They worked their way out to the main road that connected Mahogany Key with the mainland, then walked nonchalantly back to town.

Mosquitoes found them, whining. The sulfur stink of the mangroves was strong on the dark morning wind.

"I'm not going to get arrested for this, am I?"

Hawker said, "You tell me."

"I'm just a cook."

"So I've heard."

Logan looked at him strangely, then shrugged as if there was no understanding Hawker. He said, "Well, I don't care if I do. It's time we stood up to those assholes."

"Did you go the night Buck Hamilton led his raid on Chatham Harbor?"

"That was before I moved here. I've only been at the lodge for six, seven months."

"I'm sorry about Sandy." Hawker meant it.

The big man lowered his head, remembering. "Me too. I guess maybe I loved her. Funny how you find out the really important things too late."

"God likes his little jokes."

"Tell me the truth now, Hawker. Are you some kind of secret agent or something?"

"I was about to ask you the same thing, Logan."

"You know something, Hawker?"

"What's that?"

"Sometimes you really talk weird."

Logan lived in a little stilt shack near the bay. Hawker left him there, then walked to Winnie Tiger's cottage. He had promised her he would get back as soon as he could. There was a light on in the living room. He could see her through the window. She was reading. He tapped softly on the screen door, but it startled her anyway.

She pulled open the door and fell into his arms. "God, I thought you'd never get here."

He held her tight against him, her head under his chin. He could smell the shampoo odor of her hair, and her skin was warm through his sweater. She wore only a long football jersey, number 37. She tilted her head, and he looked deeply into her dark Indian eyes. "I didn't want to be alone," she whispered. "You were gone so long . . . I was worried about you. They'll come after you next . . . oh, James, they'll try to kill you next . . ."

"They've already tried to kill me."

Her eyes widened.

"They rigged my car with a bomb."

"But how did you know? What did you do with it?"

She kept brushing his neck with her lips as she talked. Hawker had his face buried in her hair. Imperceptibly, her back arched, holding the heat of her thighs against his leg.

Hawker felt his abdomen draw tense with wanting. She held his chin in her hand for a moment, eyes suddenly glassy. Her face had flushed, and her lips were moist and swollen. "The bomb," she whispered. "What did you do with . . . with . . . with the bomb?"

Hawker found her lips with his, kissing her gently. His hand slid up the soft curvature of ribs and over the full, pointed weight of her breasts. She trembled as if suddenly chilled, and moaned softly.

"Oh, God," she said. "Oh, God . . ."

"Winnie . . . listen to me. It may be better if we stop right here and go our own ways, because—"

Grinning vampishly, she grabbed a fistful of hair and pulled his lips hard against hers, her mouth open, hips pressing. Her breath was hot and sweet, and she was shaking. "Oh, James, I want you now. Now. Please, now . . ."

He lifted her into his arms, kissing her, and carried her to the bedroom. In a strange way he could understand what she was feeling. Seeing the brutalized body of Sandy Rand had been one kind of ultimate reality. There was now the need to cleanse the horror with another reality, a reality equally basic and primal, like an affirmation of life.

Hawker remembered something he'd read about the almost irresistible urge to copulate in London bomb shelters during the German air-raid blitzes.

"I want the light on," she said. "I want to see you naked—again."

At the bed, she stood and pulled the sweater over his head. She traced a vertical line down his chest with her tongue, then slid his jeans away as he pulled the football jersey off her. Her breasts were heavy and firm above bikini panties, with nipples long and erect on the dark expanse of areola.

Her smile was dreamy. "You look better than I remembered."

"And you look even better than I imagined."

She looked at him, eyes wide with mock concern. "My God, man, do you have a permit for that thing?"

"It's not even registered."

"You look like a signpost."

"Need directions, lady?"

She slid to her knees, kissing him. "Urn . . . I guess I better read the label, huh? They're usually . . . on . . . the back . . ."

Hawker's hands clenched into fists; his eyes closed. When he could stand it no longer, he swung her onto the bed and stripped her panties away. She was breathing heavily, as if she had just run a long distance. Her hips arched rhythmically, open to him, and moist.

"Now," she gasped. "Please, James, I can't wait any longer. Please, now . . ."

He touched his tongue to her dark pubic hair, smiling. She smelled warm and sweet. "My turn to read the label," he whispered.

She shuddered. "Oh, I can't stand it . . . *yes* . . . please, take me . . . *yes* . . . inside me, please, please, please . . . God, what a cruel smile you have, you *bastard!*"

"Label's got to be here somewhere," said James Hawker, his voice muffled. "Just want to see what I'm getting into . . ."

Hawker awoke to the distant propeller rumble of an airplane starting, and then the bullwhip *ker-wack* and thunder of an explosion.

The ground shook. Windows rattled. Birds screamed in the trees.

It was 11:45 A.M.

Naked, Dr. Winnie Tiger braced herself on one elbow. Her blue-black hair hung in a veil over half her face and onto her right breast. She swept the hair away with her right hand.

"We sent it back to them," said Hawker. He threw the covers aside and stood looking out the window. There was a corona of yellow light above the pine trees near the airstrip.

The Indian woman nodded sleepily, not understanding. Her eyes asked a question.

"The bomb," Hawker said. "You asked what we did with the bomb they put in my car." Hawker pulled the curtains away from the window for a better look. He wished he were at Chatham Harbor to see how the Colombians were reacting. It was important to know how disciplined they were.

He turned and looked at the woman. The beauty of her made him ache. He stepped into his jeans and reached for his sweater. "Around here you get overnight delivery with airmail," he said, leaving.

FOURTEEN

Hawker figured it would take about forty-eight hours for Medelli to get his business finished, refuel the yacht, take on provisions and sail for the anonymity of the Gulf of Mexico.

The Colombians, he knew, would be burning the entire time to take revenge on Mahogany Key for the killing of Pedro Cartagena and for the bombing of their plane.

Medelli would condone the retaliation, but he wouldn't want to be around to see it. People in the diplomatic service don't mind brutality as long as it can't be traced back to them.

At least that was what Hawker hoped. He needed the forty-eight hours, desperately needed them. And so did the town. They all had a lot of preparing to do.

Hawker worked at the computer inside his cottage. Outside the townspeople worked at the restoration of the Tarpon Inn. Hammers and lumber *whammed, whacked;* men shouted orders, and there was the grind and hydraulic whine of a backhoe.

The landscaping was almost done. They had planted a hedge

maze of jasmine and little oasis islands of coconut palms with fountains.

The whole parking lot had been screened by yellow-bloomed oleander and red hibiscus.

The new marina manager had replaced all the metal signs with hand-chiseled wooden signs, and he had re-sided the grim cement marina office with cypress planking that had been worn to silver during its years as a fishing shack.

The work was only three-quarters completed, but the Tarpon Inn Lodge had never looked better. The outside had been scraped, sanded and sprayed with bleach and water to kill mildew, then painted a bright sailing-schooner white. The hurricane shutters were green.

Earlier that afternoon, walking from Winnie Tiger's cottage, Hawker had seen Harley Bates, their fishing guide, returning from an early charter. With him was Peter Barrett, executive editor of *Field and Stream*. Bates carried a snook in each hand, struggling beneath the weight of them. Barrett was grinning as he took pictures.

Word was getting out about Mahogany Key's Tarpon Inn. And it was spreading fast. It would take another few seasons before the work they were doing now would really begin to pay off, but it was a start. Winnie had come up with the idea of slipping word to a national feminist group—through an anonymous letter, perhaps—that the owner of the Tarpon Inn had vowed he'd sell the place before he would allow women to enter the sacred confines of his fishing and hunting club bar. They would get national publicity from that, and Winnie guessed—

correctly—that the barons of industry and business from all over the country would stand in line to join.

So things were going as planned. So far. Hawker had been a cop too long not to know that just when things seem their smoothest, alarms start going off, and even the best plans can crumble.

Hawker hunched over his computer, damn well determined to make his first assignment from Jacob Montgomery Hayes a success. He had worked too hard to see the plans fall apart. Not now. He liked the people of Mahogany Key too well. And Medelli and his left-wing politicos were long overdue for a fall.

The first thing he did was get a telephone hookup with Comp-U-Serve, a general information data center in California. The computer there questioned him in lime-green letters on his own video screen. He wanted: (1) general—South America; (2) specific—political; (3) specific—guerrilla armies; (4) specific—Tigre squad.

The computer didn't have much, but it had enough. The menu offered him a partial chapter from a master's thesis on Guatemalan politics, a variety of short news stories (two from the Chicago papers, which mentioned the Tigre squad in relation to the murder of young Jake Hayes), and an excellent translation from a Bogotá political journal that had in-depth information on the guerrilla army.

Hawker skimmed through them all but settled on the Bogotá journal. Three things caught his attention.

One was the paragraph: "The Tigre squad is a paramilitary organization that recruits in small numbers throughout South and Central America. Membership seems to be based loosely on racial criteria, with strong Indio-Spanish backgrounds favored, and an absolute, near-religious dedication to the cause. As stated many times in Tigre squad literature, their ultimate aim is the infiltration and overthrow of Anglo-influenced governments through coercion, violence and economic sabotage."

The two other items that caught Hawker's attention were names. They were the same names he had found in the address section of the dead Colombian's billfold: Medelli and Guillermo.

Anton Nuñez Guillermo, though he was never personally associated with the Tigre squad, had, apparently, written a passionate pseudopolitical religious monograph while in college that the Tigre organization had adopted as its bible. Guillermo, it seemed, was half political hero, half god.

Hawker cleared with Comp-U-Serve and made two phone calls.

First he called a Mafioso acquaintance of his, Louis Brancacci, in Chicago. Like many cops, Hawker had found it necessary to court underworld connections to aid him in his police work.

Brancacci was a soft crime baron in south Chicago. He ran numbers rackets and gambling houses, all catering to old money and the upper middle class. Brancacci refused to deal with poor blue collar slobs determined to gamble away the grocery money. As he had pointed out to Hawker more than once in comic earnest, no one respected the American family more than he. Brancacci was a crook. But he was a crook with morals. And that was more than Hawker could say for many of the law-abiding politicians he had met.

"Hawker," exclaimed the distant voice. "How's my favorite cop? Or should I say ex-cop?" The high machine-gun-clatter laugh sounded like it was coming from Mars. Hawker could picture Brancacci sitting in his comfortable den in his comfortable Cicero suburban home, feet up, white silk tie knotted on dark shirt, drinking fruit juice and watching a ball game.

"Need some information, Louie."

"Ha! And why should I help? You're not a cop anymore, right?"

"Because we're friends, Louie. Besides, it's got nothing to do with you or anybody in your little boys' club back home. There's a guy in Washington, a diplomat—a Colombian named Guillermo. Can you find out if your people have had any dealings with him?"

"Sure, Hawk, sure. May take me a couple of phone calls—but you're going to owe me one for it. Ask those East Coast boys for a small favor and they hold it over your head like they saved your old lady from drowning."

"I'll let you win at racquetball next time we play."

"You're becoming a real human being, Hawker. They ought to give medals."

"Can you call me tonight?"

"Yeah, where are you? The old cops' retirement home? Ha!"

Hawker and Brancacci talked for a while longer, then Hawker tried the little two-room police station on Mahogany Key. Chief Ben Simps didn't answer. He finally reached him on the phone at his luxury houseboat.

"Simps? Hawker. I want to see you this afternoon. Alone."

"Can't this afternoon, Hawker. I'm just getting ready to go out in my boat. I'm going to anchor off White Horse Key and do a little fishing. I'll be back in three days. By then the FAA boys will be done with their investigation of that plane explosion. I don't want to answer any questions about that, Hawker."

"Have you called them yet?"

Simps hesitated. "No. I had a feeling you'd be calling me first. You did it, didn't you? You blew up the plane."

Hawker ignored the question. "I'll see you this afternoon, Simps. Not in three days. Understand? I'll meet you at the station at five. Be there."

Hawker hung up before Simps could reply.

Using the Visicalc program, Hawker turned once again to his computer. He wanted to enter all the random data he had and set up an orderly system of graphs that, he hoped, would give him a group of probabilities. Hawker had information, but he had no answers. He hoped the computer would provide some.

It didn't.

He worked until the sweat beaded on his forehead. He entered a datum, reentered it, swore at the computer, and only the expense of the unit saved it from being slapped, banged and abused.

Working on the premise that the computer is never wrong, Hawker decided he either didn't have enough data or he was setting up his probability graphs incorrectly. Sometimes the computer made Hawker feel downright dumb. He was about to call Timothy Hoffacker, his computer-whiz friend, when a knock at the door interrupted him.

The massive shape of Logan loomed outside. He stepped in, looking sheepish and pleased. His dark beard had been combed, and he wore clean clothes.

"Glad I wasn't on the noon flight out of Mahogany Key," he said with a smile.

"How many Colombians were on the plane?"

"One. A guy named Velindez. I'd seen him around. Tough guy. Liked to throw his weight around. I wasn't here, but I heard he and a couple of his buddies beat one of the crabbers half to death their second month in town." Logan's eyes narrowed to slits. "They didn't find much of him."

"From the sound of the explosion, I'm surprised they found anything at all. You know your explosives."

"I'm just a cook."

"I need to write that down someplace. I keep forgetting."

"I came to talk to you about the men—the men working on the lodge. Just about every man in town, in fact. They know about Sandy's murder, and they know how she died. She was well liked in this town. Grew up here. They were calling for Colombian blood this morning. But they were still a little scared. You know about the last time they went to Chatham Harbor?"

"Yeah," said Hawker. "I know."

"They're not dumb. They figure you or I had something to do with that plane blowing up—mostly, they figure it was you. A couple of the boys came to me during lunch hour. They want you to lead them on another raid. They want another chance to clean out the Colombians. They said they're going no matter what. But they'd rather have you leading them."

Hawker shook his head. "It can't be me. It has to be one of their own. If I provide the courage while I'm here, then they'll figure the courage leaves when I leave."

"You're going?" Logan eyed him shrewdly. "After all the work you've done getting this lodge fixed up, why would you leave? You are the new owner, aren't you?"

"I think you know better than that," Hawker said softly.

Logan said nothing for a long minute. Finally he nodded. "Yeah," he said. "Yeah, I guess I did know." He turned to go, but stopped at the door. "Oh, by the way, quite a few of the boys want to take the afternoon off."

"Christ, they don't want to go after the Colombians already, do they? Tell them they ought to do it tomorrow night. Hell, lack of planning is what killed them the last time, and by then I should have just the guy to lead—"

Logan was laughing. "Yes, they're eager to go after the Colombians. But they're more eager to do something else."

"What's that?"

"When the plane blew up, you know what came pouring down like rain? Money. Beautiful money. Twenties, fifties and hundreds, mostly. The stuff is thick out there in the mangroves. I even noticed a few bills stuck in the live oak outside your cottage. They want the afternoon off so they can go money hunting."

Hawker was suddenly deep in thought. The paragraph from the Bogotá journal kept buzzing through his brain, as elusive as an answer to a very complex problem. That was when it finally dawned on him—

"Hawk! Did you hear me?" Logan was looking at him strangely. "What about the men? Can they have the afternoon off?"

"What? Oh, yeah. Tell them to take the afternoon off. And tell them they'll get their second chance at the Colombians. There'll be a meeting at the lodge tonight—midnight."

When Logan had gone, Hawker sat in meditation for a time. He was sure he was right. It explained almost everything.

He made two more phone calls, then worked at the computer for another long hour, using the RUSTLED software to plant a bogus career record under his name in some very important computer banks.

That done, he dialed Eastern Airlines in Miami and made reservations on the midnight flight to Washington, D.C.

There were still a few things he had to do. The second was to visit Boggs McKay, Mahogany Key's star athlete and born leader, now turned hermit.

The first was to find a ladder.

FIFTEEN

Boggs McKay lived in a platform house on an acre of salt-beaten land on the bank of the Chatham River.

Chickens scavenged among the weeds. Rusted car parts, broken chairs and other junk spilled out of the shed. The house was of warped gray planking with a tin roof, and there were no curtains on the windows. A potbellied horse dozed in the shade of a black mangrove, its tail swatting mosquitoes.

You could smell the river from the long dirt road that led to the house.

Two pointers roared at Hawker from beneath an old blue Chevy pickup. Hawker stopped and held his hands out for inspection. The pointers sniffed him, urinated on the tires of his Monte Carlo as if in warning, then stalked back to their beds beneath the truck. The dogs looked healthy: good coats, clear eyes, and they carried the right amount of weight. Hawker took it as a good sign. McKay obviously still cared about something.

"Out back!" yelled a voice. "Out here by the boat. Come around."

Boggs McKay kneeled on the deck of a forty-plus-foot

wooden crabber. The wheelhouse was built forward, with VHF and loran antennae mounted above. He was working on one of the two stern-mounted winches, grease up to his elbows.

He looked up as Hawker approached and shook his head. "I told you on the phone I didn't want to talk to you."

As on the phone, something in McKay's voice told Hawker just the opposite—he did want to talk. He did want to help. But it was going to take some prodding. The right kind of prodding. Hawker remembered what Buck Hamilton had said about Boggs McKay not following anyone anywhere.

"I'm persistent," said Hawker, smiling brightly. "You have to give me that."

McKay nodded and said nothing. He was a heavily muscled, middle-size man in his late thirties. His hair was cropped short, redder than Hawker's, and you could see the stomach muscle patchwork beneath a thin layer of fat. He had kept himself in shape.

Despite the grease and sweat, McKay had the studious, intelligent face of a college student grown older. Hawker could picture the way he must have been as a businessman: a good handshake, an honest smile and fierce, predatory eyes that must have made his competitors wince and his employees jump. Hawker decided he wasn't the kind of man who could be manipulated. He didn't try.

"You know why I'm here, Boggs. You probably even know what I'm going to say. So tell me: are you going to play deaf and dumb all afternoon, or are we going to talk?"

Boggs McKay turned from his work and surveyed Hawker with a pair of searing blue eyes. Hawker didn't intimidate easily, but McKay was coming as close as anyone. Hawker realized that a man like McKay would have to test him before he was about to make any commitments.

McKay stood, grabbed a towel and jumped down onto the dock, wiping his hands. His eyes never left Hawker. The width of his shoulders made him look deceptively short. He walked down the dock to the yard, then stopped an arm's length away, eye to eye. "You're right," he said sharply. "I do know why you're here. I've heard all about the great James Hawker. You're the one who stood up to the Colombians—a few of them, anyway. You're the smart Yankee businessman who bought the Tarpon Inn, and now you're trying to show us dumb Southerners how to get back on our feet again, right?"

Hawker smiled calmly. "I've only met one really dumb Southerner since I've been here, McKay—you."

Boggs McKay took a quick step forward, and when Hawker didn't back away, he stopped. The tough-guy facade fell away, leaving a sly smile. McKay began to laugh, softly at first, then louder and louder, like a dam breaking, tears rolling down his face. Hawker got the impression McKay hadn't laughed in a very long time. He knew why. The computer had confirmed Buck Hamilton's story about McKay's kids being killed by a drunken driver and about the broken marriage. Life, Hawker knew, could be one nasty son of a bitch. And bastards stupid enough and selfish enough to drive after drinking had done more than their share to prove it.

McKay had needed his time as a hermit, the long months alone, seething and healing both. But there has to come a moment when a person broken in spirit decides to throw open the doors of his hermitage. If he doesn't, honest mourning takes on the odor of human rot.

Hawker was betting that McKay sensed it was his time to return to the world of the living.

"Gawddamn, gawddamn," McKay said in his thick Southern drawl, still convulsed with laughter. "We're out here like two boys on the playground, seeing who'd back down first—and you wouldn't budge, by damn! Honest to god, Hawker, I pulled that on a government inspector a few years back, and he liked to piss his drawers. But not you! Hell, you're not only as ugly as me, but you're just as mean, too—" The words were lost in another gust of laughter.

"Does that mean you'll talk?"

Boggs McKay wiped his eyes with the greasy towel, sobering. "What do you have in mind, Hawker?"

"You know what I have in mind—the Colombians. One more year like the last one and there won't be any town called Mahogany Key."

"And why should I care about that?"

"Because it's time you started caring about something, Boggs."

Boggs McKay was silent for a long while. He ran a hand through his short red hair and flung sweat to the ground. Flies buzzed in the January sunlight, and chickens scratched in the sand. Finally he looked at Hawker. "Do you have some kind of plan?"

"I do. But the plan needs a leader."

"That Sandy Rand was a good girl. We used to date some in high school. She could make a man laugh till he couldn't stop."

"I didn't know her long, but I liked her," said Hawker.

McKay nodded, as if affirming something within himself. "I don't keep beer, but I've got iced tea inside. Bring those charts or maps or whatever you've got in your hand and come on in. We'll talk."

It was well after five before Hawker finished his meeting with Boggs McKay, but Chief Ben Simps was still at the little two-room police station, waiting.

The place was painted a dingy yellow, and it smelled of stale cigars. There were file cabinets, a locked gun case, a National Crime Information Center teletype and a one-man cage.

"You're late, Hawker," said Simps. He had stood up quickly when Hawker entered. He looked nervous.

From a sack Hawker took two of the seismic disks and put them on the metal desk.

"What are those? Hey—what are those things, anyway? I'm not planting any bombs, damn it—"

"They're not bombs," Hawker snapped. "You don't need to know what they are. You're going to take them to Medelli's boat tonight. You're going to hide one on the deck. Put it under the canvas of one of the Whalers. The other you're going to hide in the head. A boat that big has to have a vanity in the head. Stick it under the vanity."

"But what if I can't get on the boat—"

"Then hide them in the bathroom and the living room of the main house."

Simps was sweating. His heavy face glistened. "But Christ, what if they catch me? You don't know those guys—"

"And once you've hidden them," Hawker interrupted, "get the hell out of town. Take a cruise, drive to Miami—I don't care." Hawker turned to leave, then stopped. "And one more thing, Simps. If you double-cross us, we'll find you. You can't run far enough or hide well enough. There's nothing I hate more than a crooked cop, Simps. I'll find you myself and kill you."

Hawker slammed the door behind him and didn't look back.

SIXTEEN

Hawker returned to his cottage. The west coast of Florida was losing its daylight, and a dusk chill blew off the bay.

He set water to boiling for tea and stared at the phone, willing it to ring.

He was eager to receive the call from his Mafioso friend, Louis Brancacci.

When the phone didn't oblige, he stripped his clothes off and walked naked to the shower. The linoleum was cold.

He lathered, rinsed, then steamed for a while. When the teakettle whistled, he roughed himself dry.

Hawker pulled on a pair of soft gray tropical-worsted slacks and an oxford shirt with blue pinstripes. He hadn't brought enough socks, and he was glad the one washed pair left was the satin-soft wool. Hawker decided he wouldn't bother with the Hebrides tweed jacket until he caught the midnight plane out of Miami.

Graeme Mellor was wiping the bar when Hawker entered. "I haven't seen you that bloody well dressed since your first day in town," he said with a grin. "What's the occasion? The big town meeting tonight?"

Hawker took a seat and swallowed part of the beer Mellor had drawn. "Who told you about the meeting?"

"Logan was in here first. Then about ten minutes after he headed for the kitchen, Winnie came looking for you. Like I told you, word travels fast in this town. They both knew."

Hawker picked up a pad and wrote his supper order on it. He ripped the sheet off and handed it to the New Zealander. Mellor squinted at it, reading through his wire-rimmed glasses. Hawker noticed a small purple bruise on his cheek for the first time.

"How'd you get that?"

Mellor touched his cheek. "This?" He winced as if it hurt. "I was in here late last night, going over the books—they look better, by the way. The books look much better. Well, I was drinking a beer or two while I worked, and I guess I must have had a pint too much." He laughed and held up his hands. "Fell down the damn steps as I was leaving. Bashed my face and tore my bloody pants to boot."

Hawker laughed with him—outwardly. Inwardly he was suddenly suspicious. Maybe Logan hadn't been lying. Maybe he had been telling the truth when he said he hadn't killed the Colombian.

Hawker snapped his fingers. "Say, I think I'm going to change that supper order."

"You don't want the broiled pompano? It's awfully good baked in the brown paper bag like Logan does it."

"Naw, I think I'll have lobster. Three nice tails, say."

126

Mellor gave him a perplexed look. "We're out of lobster; you know that. It's way past season."

Hawker shook his head and winked at him. "I'm pretty sure I hid a dozen or so away in the old walk-in freezer. You know, for a special occasion. I've got to drive into Miami tonight for a meeting with some travel agents in the morning, so I guess this is special occasion enough. You help Logan look for them. You'll find them."

Mellor shrugged and headed for the kitchen. The moment he was gone, Hawker went to work. It was just a hunch, but more than once a hunch of his had saved a life.

Someone had done a very sloppy job of hiding them. It took him all of two minutes to find the first: a candy-color transmitting device with a single thin-wire antenna. The bug had a small magnet on it. It narrowed Hawker's field of search. They had to be attached to metal objects. He found two more before the creak of the kitchen door announced Mellor's return.

Mellor came out, slapping his arms as if he was freezing. "I swear there are no lobster tails back there, James. We both looked until we 'bout froze our bloody balls off. Logan says you owe him a drink. He says he's going to have to sit on the stove for an hour or two before he can use the restroom. He says even then he's going to have to goose himself in the ass and grab his plumbing when it jumps out—"

"I get the general idea," said Hawker, laughing despite himself. "Tell him I'll take the pompano. And I'll buy him his drink. Oh, and Graeme?" Hawker watched the New Zealander's eyes carefully. "Were you planning on holding tonight's meeting in the bar?"

He grinned. "You know how thirsty fishermen get when they talk. We can use the extra business."

"Have there been people in the dining room all evening?"

"Yeah. It's getting so the kitchen is pretty busy."

"Let's give the local boys a chance to see how we've fixed up the place. Hold the meeting in the dining room, okay? Besides, we don't want anybody drunk. This meeting is too important."

"Sure," said Mellor. "I hadn't thought of that."

Hawker watched the New Zealander return to the kitchen. As he sipped at his beer, he wondered who had planted the bugs: Mellor, Logan—or Winnie Tiger.

Hawker didn't see the Colombians enter the bar, but he saw Mellor's face change. His eyes widened and he grimaced. "Holy Christ," he whispered. "Someone let the animals loose."

There were two men coming through the doorway. The first was a small man, snake thin, in his late thirties or early forties. His black hair was greased back, and his narrow mustache was as shiny as his hair. He wore a white sports coat with a dark shirt and white tie. A cigarette protruded from the swarthy Latin face, making him squint. His neck and wrists were adorned with gold jewelry, and he carried a leather briefcase.

But it was the man behind him who had made Mellor grimace. He was one of the biggest human beings Hawker had ever seen.

It was the mulatto, Simio.

Simio's head was curiously elongated, like a football, and sat flush on his shoulders as if he had no neck. His face was saffron color, and he had tiny, gun-barrel-size eyes that were a chalky albino blue. The white pullover shirt strained against the sheer mass of him. His biceps were as large as most men's thighs, and his sledgelike fists hung almost to his knees. He had to duck slightly to get under the door, and his shaved head barely cleared the ceiling fans. He had to be close to seven feet tall. The expression on his face was that of a pit bulldog trotting toward a fight—half snarl, half grin.

"You want me to go get some help?" Mellor whispered nervously.

"Logan might be handy to have around."

"Hoo! After that freezer business, he's going to really be pissed off about this."

"What about a gun? Isn't there a gun behind the bar?"

Mellor rolled his eyes. "To kill that monster, you'd have to hack his head off, then hide it."

"Thanks."

The snake-thin Colombian swung the briefcase onto the bar. Simio stood directly behind him, his albino eyes blinking with reptilian frequency.

"My name's Medelli," said the smaller man in a thick Spanish accent. "I understand the place is under new management. Who's the owner?"

Graeme Mellor pointed and said quickly, "He is."

Hawker smiled. "That's right," he said. "I'm the new owner. What can I do for you?"

Medelli walked the briefcase down the bar and stood in front of Hawker. Simio still shadowed him. "I didn't catch your name," he said.

"I didn't drop it."

The narrow lips curled around the cigarette. Hawker guessed he was smiling. "A joke, that is correct? You are making the joke?" He looked up at Simio and said something in rapid Spanish. The mulatto's nose flattened as he hacked out deep laughter. Hawker could smell his breath: onions and stale grease.

"That is very nice," said Medelli. His eyes narrowed, thin and brutal. "We have had a little joke. Among new friends, eh?" He swung his head at Mellor. "We have business to discuss. Perhaps we might have some privacy, yes?"

"I'm staying," Mellor said firmly.

Hawker smiled at him. "No, you're not. You go on back and help Logan in the kitchen." He looked at the two Colombians. "If these boys give me any trouble, I'll toss them out myself."

The mulatto didn't understand English, but he sensed that his boss had somehow been offended. He grunted and took a step toward Hawker, but Medelli stopped him. "Another joke, eh? You are quite the funny man. But I have come here on business. Perhaps we can be done with the jokes now, eh?"

Hawker motioned the New Zealander away, and Medelli followed Hawker to a booth. Simio remained standing. Hawker ignored his glare, sipping easily at his beer. "You want to talk?" he said. "You have ten minutes. Talk."

Medelli nodded, his fingers making piano exercise movements on the briefcase. "You are a blunt man. I like that, for I, too, am a blunt man. Perhaps we are alike in other ways. I am a man who has his way. It is my *orgullo*—my pride, you might say. People who work with me are treated fairly." He leaned toward Hawker slightly. "People who get in my way are crushed."

"You're wasting time, Medelli. Eight minutes."

The Colombian nodded, his face slowly paling with anger. He dropped all pretension. "Then I will be frank. I want to buy the Tarpon Inn, Mr. Whoever-you-are. No, let me say that in another way, eh? I am *going* to buy the Tarpon Inn." He clicked the briefcase open and swung it around toward Hawker. It was full of money in crisp stacks. The stacks were banded in brown paper: hundred-dollar bills.

"I am going to pay you five hundred thousand dollars for the land, the buildings—everything. How do you say it in America—'cash money'?"

Hawker smiled. "I paid seven hundred thousand. I wouldn't be much of a businessman if I took a two-hundred-thousand loss after all the work I've done."

Medelli's index finger tapped the table angrily. "I will give you a million, then. I will be back with the money tonight."

Hawker shook his head. "The place is worth five times that."

"Five million dollars?" The Colombian's face was turning red. With obvious effort he forced himself to remain calm. He took a deep breath. "All right, then. I will give you five million dollars. But not tonight. We are leaving very late tomorrow, and I will return in two weeks. I will bring the money then." He paused. "But we will sign the papers now. Tonight. I have brought papers with me."

"In two weeks the price will be higher—all the improvements we're making, you know. Inflation."

It happened very quickly. Too quickly. Medelli slammed the briefcase shut, and suddenly Hawker was looking into the barrel of a tiny chrome automatic. "You will sign the papers now!" he hissed. "Do you understand? This moment!"

Hawker made a noncommittal shrug and reached for the pen the Colombian had produced. Halfway across the table, he backhanded the pistol to the floor and hit Medelli with a glancing left that jolted his mouth open—and suddenly Hawker was airborne.

As if in slow motion, he felt himself spinning across the room. He hit with a bone-jarring thud, and then used the bar as a brace to pull himself to his feet.

Simio was coming at him, the tiny albino eyes blazing.

The mulatto tried to grab him, but Hawker ducked beneath the massive arms and hit him three quick shots in the kidneys. Simio roared, turned and swung. Hawker blocked the punch with his forearm, but the impact of it sent him skidding across the floor. Medelli, he noticed absently, was still sitting dazed at the table.

The mulatto came at him in another charge. Instead of letting himself be backed against the wall, Hawker stepped through his arms and peppered him with a series of cutting jabs. It stopped his momentum. Hawker drove his left fist as hard as he could into the giant's side, then put all his weight behind an overhand right that crushed the flat nose flatter.

Hawker had never hit anyone harder in his life. The punch numbed his fingers and sent an electric pain up his arm.

The mulatto took two quick steps backward, shaking his head. Then he grinned at Hawker and spat blood at him.

Hawker was trying to decide between lunging for the automatic on the floor—and risking having his back broken—or jumping over the bar in search of a knife when Logan and Graeme Mellor burst into the room, each holding shotguns.

"*Hold it!*"

The mulatto studied the guns for a moment, growled at the men holding them, spat some more blood at Hawker, then shrugged. Slowly, as if he was used to having weapons pointed at him, he lifted Medelli over his shoulder, took the briefcase and lumbered through the door.

He didn't look back.

Hawker shook his head, still a little in awe, and sat down heavily on a bar stool. "Jesus, what took you guys so long?"

"How about a beer?" Mellor asked. "A cool beer, and some ice for that hand?"

"We couldn't find any weapons in the lodge," said Logan. "The carpenters are redoing the billiards room, and they'd stored the gun case upstairs."

Mellor brought a champagne bucket full of ice, and Hawker buried his right fist in it. "You could have come with clubs, damn it. Clubs are easy to find."

"That guy's awful big," Mellor reasoned.

"A lot bigger than me," put in Logan. He smiled. "Besides, we'd both heard you were pretty good with your fists, and we wanted to see how good."

"Very impressive it was, too," said Mellor with a sniff.

"You two assholes stood and watched!"

"Just the last five minutes, boss. Hey, how about another beer? I'd like one. Logan, why don't we all have another nice cold beer . . ."

Back in his cottage, Hawker stripped his clothes off and dropped his ruined shirt in the trash.

It was 10:05 P.M.

He didn't have much time to get to Miami International.

The telephone rang while he was in the shower. It was the call he had been waiting for. It was Louis Brancacci.

"Hawk, where the hell have you been? I musta called a dozen times."

"What did you find out, Louie?"

"That friend of yours in Washington—Guillermo?"

"Yeah."

"No straight information, but some rumors and some good guesses. It's serious stuff. You want it over the phone? I've got a friend or two in Miami who wouldn't mind meeting you. They could pass on the info, one on one."

"I need the information now, Louie."

"Okay, here it is. This Guillermo is a very clever fellow. Like I said, nothing works directly through him. He's got a little organization of his own in D.C., and it stinks from the ground floor up. He's into a lot of things—has to be, because they have one hell of a cash flow. Drugs, for one. Maybe illegal weaponry, maybe some extortion. Since he's a diplomat, the money laundry is very clean—foreigners can bring all the money they want *into* the country, and they don't have to account for the source. Sweet, huh? I almost admire the guy."

"What kind of drugs, Louie?"

"The kind of stuff that travels easy and sells big, I suppose."

"Cocaine and heroin?"

"That would be my guess. And they must be bringing in tons of it, because the organization is very, very fat. Buying up all kinds of stuff. Heavy cash nut—so heavy, I'm surprised the feds haven't got him. Hell, those boys aren't dumb." He chuckled. "Well, not too dumb, anyway. Stands to reason they'd have found a way to sneak a look at his luggage, diplomatic immunity or not."

"Have your people figured in any of the exchanges?"

"Nope. Of course, I would tell you no anyway, but this time I happen to mean it. Like I said, it's rumor and guesswork."

"That helps me, Louie. It adds some important pieces to the puzzle. His people have been carrying around suitcases full of money down here, and one of his lieutenants just offered me five times what my new fishing lodge is worth and didn't blink an eye."

"Fishing lodge? You? Hey, how about filling me in, Hawk? Don't you think I deserve an explanation? I've got all of two long distance phone calls invested—no, make that three. The area code you gave me says you're someplace in sunny Florida. How is it down there?"

"Sunny," said Hawker. "Don't forget—you win at racquetball next time."

"What a guy . . ."

SEVENTEEN

Encased in an aluminum tube of narrow seats, smiling stewardesses, canned oxygen and club sandwiches, Hawker jetted from the Gulf Stream balm of Miami to the slush-freeze and smog of Washington, D.C.

At thirty thousand feet the cold lights of the Atlantic seaboard peeled away beneath him: the nestled glimmer of mountain villages, the neon sprawl of industrial slums, then the Capitol building domed in light and the white obelisk of the Washington Monument.

There was the Goodyear screech, the rumble of reversed engines and the audible sighs of seven dozen souls happy to have survived, smokers and nonsmokers.

It was 2:15 A.M.

Hawker could feel the seepage of arctic air through the exit tunnel. People in the terminal wore coats and gloves. They looked unhappy. They looked in a hurry.

Hawker bought a *New York Times*, folded it beneath his arm and found the information desk on the main floor—all as he

136

had been instructed to do. The counter was closed. Hawker put the duffel bag at his feet and waited.

"Mr. Thornton?" asked a man. He wore an Austrian hat with fur lining. He was in his late fifties, and he looked like he probably owned a Mercedes and kept dachshunds.

Jacob Montgomery Hayes had given the man the proper alias. Thornton was Hawker's middle name, his late mother's maiden name.

"Yes?"

"My name is . . . Schmidt."

Clever, thought Hawker. "You were to arrange an appointment for me," he said.

The man nodded quickly. Mr. Schmidt was obviously playing an unfamiliar role. Hawker wondered who he really was and how Hayes had gotten him. "I contacted Mr. Guillermo's office," Schmidt said. "They said he had a very full schedule in the morning."

"That's what we expected him to say."

The man nodded again. "I did just as our mutual friend suggested I do. I told them it was a matter of the greatest importance. I stressed that several times."

"And?"

"And I gave them the telephone number of the room I've reserved for you. They asked for your full name. Twice."

"Good," said Hawker. "Good."

"Did you bring the money?"

Hawker fished two hundred-dollar bills, two fifties and two twenties out of his inside jacket pocket. Mr. Schmidt seemed unhappy that they were making the transaction so openly.

"Are you with the Federal Reserve?"

"Really, Mr. Thornton, that shouldn't concern you."

"Just call me nosy. And you'll be telephoning me?"

"That was our agreement."

"Tomorrow?"

"This sort of thing takes time. There are tests to be done, with chemicals and a microscope—"

"It has to be tomorrow. You have the number in Florida?"

"Of course."

"No later than seven P.M., Mr. . . . . Schmidt."

"I can only do my best, Mr. Thornton," muttered the man. "I can only do my best." He pivoted and marched away down the long corridor, walking strangely like a penguin.

Hawker couldn't resist. He called after him, "Mr. Schmidt—I was just wondering. Do you own dachshunds?"

The man studied him for a moment, as if Hawker might be joking. Finally he said, "Dobermans, Mr. Thornton. I keep two of them. I gave my dear little dachshunds away when I moved to this godforsaken town."

Mr. Schmidt turned and disappeared among the cloaked and hurrying travelers.

Guillermo's office telephoned just after ten A.M.

Hawker had almost given up hope. He had spent the morning trying to entertain himself in his room at the Stradford Hotel.

He had done push-ups, finished one of Allan W. Eckert's fine pieces on natural history, then done more push-ups.

Desperate, he finally turned on the television.

He was watching John Wayne in *The Quiet Man* when the telephone rang. It was one of Hawker's favorite movies, but the color was bad. John Wayne had a green face, and Maureen O'Hara's hair was harlot orange.

It was sacrilege.

Hawker switched off the television and answered the phone.

"Mr. Thornton, please."

"I'm Thornton."

"James H. Thornton?" It was a woman. Her secretarial formality didn't hide the Spanish accent.

"Yes."

"Mr. Guillermo will be happy to see you this morning, Mr. Thornton. If it's convenient for you, Mr. Guillermo would be pleased if you would meet him at the Hyde Street Diplomat's Club."

"Where? The lounge?"

He could tell the woman was smiling. "In the steam room, Mr. Thornton. We have called ahead and arranged your pass. Just give them your name at the desk. Is eleven all right?"

"Fine," said Hawker.

He jotted down directions, then called Washington International Airport and made reservations on the 2:30 P.M. flight back to Miami. He showered, put on fresh clothes, knotted a British regimental tie in the mirror, packed his duffel bag and paid his bill.

Washington was in the grip of a cold front. Outside, ash-color snow squeaked under his feet, and the air burned his throat. His breath fogged and his eyes watered.

People on the streets walked with their heads down, hats

breaking the cold before them. Hawker fell into line, surprised that during his weeks in Florida he had lost the fast-paced gait of the city pedestrian.

At a bank with mirrored windows. Hawker stopped as if adjusting his tie.

The car that had followed him from the airport—a black, official-looking Chevrolet—was having a tough time following him now. Traffic was fast, and the car was moving slowly, matching his walk. Horns blared. A taxi driver flashed a finger angrily at the two men inside.

Hawker had plenty of time to get to the Hyde Street Diplomat's Club. He had nothing to lose by being followed, but he didn't like it. He turned in at a coffee shop beside the bank and made a phone call. Working as a Chicago cop, he had heard plenty such calls, and he had no trouble giving his voice the proper mixture of outrage and fear.

The black Chevy sat outside, double-parked. Hawker ordered tea and waited.

It didn't take long for the Washington cops to arrive. The blue light of their squad car *popped-pulsed*. A backup car skidded to a halt behind. Four officers jumped out, revolvers ready. Cops, Hawker knew, welcome the chance to stop a bank robbery before it occurs.

Hawker paid his bill and stepped outside. The sky was gray, and snow was falling. The cops had the two men against the Chevy, frisking them. The men were stripped of their weapons.

One of the men—a lanky man with an Abe Lincoln face—glared at Hawker.

Hawker smiled. He gave him a short salute and walked on.

*   *   *

The Hyde Park Diplomat's Club was a severe brown-stone with a brass nameplate. The doorman wore a uniform.

Hawker was given a guest pass and a key to a locker. The dressing rooms were plush: red leather furniture, blue carpeting. There were fruit juice and mineral water dispensers in the lounge, and three television sets. Two of them were tuned to stock market reports, the other to an empty congressional meeting room.

The walls were lined with twenty-four-hour military clocks, showing time around the world. Hawker noted that Colombia was an hour behind Washington.

It was 10:58 A.M.

Except for two men dressing for handball, Hawker was alone. He locked his clothes away and carried his towel and razor into the glass and redwood steam room. He pulled the chain, squirting water on the rocks.

He had almost Finished shaving when a face pressed against the window. The door opened, and a fully clothed figure appeared through the swirling steam.

"Mr. Thornton?"

"In the flesh."

The figure didn't smile. It pulled off its gloves and peered under both decks of the steam room and into the heating unit. Guillermo wasn't dumb. A person can't carry a wire—a tape recorder or a transmitting unit—into a steam room, but it can be hidden there. Now he was having one of his goons check the place out.

"Would you mind standing, Mr. Thornton?"

141

Hawker stood.

"Remove the towel and turn around, please."

Hawker stood and turned.

"Now if you will kindly bend over—"

Hawker reached the figure in two steps, grabbed him by the collar and wedged his thumb and forefinger under the man's jaw, then slammed him against the wall.

"I think that's enough Simon Says for one morning, asshole. Now go send your boss in here like a good boy."

The man's hand moved toward the shoulder holster inside his jacket. Hawker slapped him twice and took the automatic. It was a German-made parabellum. The man struggled to free himself, and Hawker applied more pressure with his thumb and forefinger.

It had a calming effect.

"Trouble, gentlemen?"

A rotund man with a gray wreath of hair appeared through the steam. His skin was the color of fresh mahogany and baby smooth, and his belly hung over blue boxer-type bathing shorts. There was a suggestion of the Mayan in the craggy nose and hollowed cheeks, but the brown eyes had a St. Nicholas crinkle, and his gray mustache gave him a grandfatherly look.

Hawker had expected an entirely different sort of man.

"Guillermo?"

"*Mr.* Guillermo, if you don't mind, Mr. Thornton. Allow me my prefix, please."

"I think you have a candidate for AIDS disease here."

Guillermo's face assumed a tisk-tisk expression. "You may go now, Hans. Oh, and Mr. Thornton has taken your weapon, has he? That is bad, Hans. We must have a little talk—but later."

There was only a hint of sharpness in the South American's voice, but Hawker felt the bodyguard wince as if he had been whipped. He released him and handed the automatic to Guillermo. The steam room door closed softly.

"A thorough people, the Germans," said the older man, arranging himself on the lower deck. He considered the automatic he held, then placed it on the redwood bench, away from Hawker. "One might expect two generations of living in South America to soften them a bit. But blood runs deep in such a people. Frankly, many of us were surprised they lost the war." He chuckled. "The utter temerity of it—a nation smaller than this country's Florida challenging and nearly defeating the entire modern world." His chuckle became a smile. "You are from Florida, Mr. Thornton. And you have come a very long way to see me. Why, I can't imagine."

"No? Then I'm surprised you agreed to a meeting. You know nothing about me."

"Come, come, Mr. Thornton. I do so tire of the diplomat's curse: the constant thrust and parry of language." He made an embracing gesture with his arms. "This is the one place in Washington where one may be completely and totally honest. The mind boggles at some of the conversations which have taken place in the security of this little room." His brown eyes burned into Hawker's. "So let's be frank, man. You know very well my people have had your background completely checked—and an intriguing background it is."

Hawker had made the fake background information as intriguing as he could on his computer back on Mahogany Key.

"I'm sure the files available even to a man in your position are limited," said Hawker baitingly.

"Don't be so sure, Mr. Thornton." Guillermo waved one finger in the air, like a professor emphasizing a particularly telling point. "For instance, I know that you worked as both a bodyguard and an assassin for the Central Intelligence Agency—no, don't look noncommittal, for I know it's true. I also know you fell from grace with the organization. The circumstances might appear mysterious to the untrained eye, but I suspect you were indulging in a bit of smuggling during your world travels. No? I think so. And then that business of your being linked to the Communist Party—the Soviets, no less! Bravo!" The man laughed appreciatively. "Is it possible there are two James H. Thorntons? No, there is the bullet wound on your thigh, the appendix scar, and the knife scar—ah, you've added another to your collection." The man presented him with a fatherly smile. "So tell me, how could I refuse an audience with one of the most intriguing Americans I've come across in many years? Especially when there is the possibility you may ask for employment. Not that I could hire you, understand. But I know certain people who might."

Hawker shook his head. "I stopped working for other people years ago. It's not a job I want. It's business. Your business."

Guillermo raised his eyebrows. "And what business might that be?"

"You're the one who suggested we be frank, Mr. Guillermo. So I will be. I know all about your operation on Mahogany Key."

Hawker watched the man's face change; watched the smile melt; watched the jowls go slack; watched the dark eyes grow cold, malevolent and deadly. "I have no idea what you're talking about," he said in a near-whisper.

"You do. But you have nothing to fear from me. I know that you're shipping in drugs. You have an organization down there run by an aide of yours named Medelli."

Slowly, ever so slowly, the smile returned to Guillermo's face. "Drugs, is it?" he said, suddenly comfortable again. "And how did you come to that conclusion?"

"I had the same idea. I wanted to find the ideal place for maximum security trafficking. I don't like risks. I'm a very careful man." Hawker shrugged. "When I settled on Mahogany Key, there was only one problem—your people already controlled it. But then I started thinking. I realized it might actually be to our mutual advantage. Why not work together? I bought a fishing lodge down there under the name of James Hawker. I have a few ideas—good ideas—about the import business, and I was hoping to have a nice discussion with this Medelli character."

"I have no idea what you're talking about," Guillermo said, smiling. "But it is an interesting tale. Please continue."

"You know exactly what I'm talking about, Mr. Guillermo. Last night Medelli came to me with one of his goons. With a couple of my employees present, he tried to force me into selling my fishing lodge. The fool even pulled a gun on me. It was then I decided that I didn't want to deal with anyone that stupid. I had already done some checking. I figured I would be better off making my offer directly to the head man." Hawker's eyes narrowed. "Here I am, Mr. Guillermo. Is the head man interested in talking?"

The older South American tapped his fingers on the redwood bench. Finally he said, "If I did know what you're talking about, Mr. Thornton—and I'm not saying I do—why should

I offer such a valuable concession to a complete stranger?" He smiled. "I am a diplomat, you see. One does not simply give valuable information away. One trades information. You come with the offer of 'business.' If, as you say, I have taken the risk of running a drug trafficking operation, then you must also assume I already have business. No? This little meeting has been interesting, but I'm afraid—"

"I have information," Hawker inserted calmly. He had anticipated that Guillermo would demand just such an exchange. "I have information you badly need. Information that could save your career, not to mention keep you out of a federal prison."

Guillermo raised his eyebrows. "By all means, tell me, Mr. Thornton. Give me this earthshaking information."

"If you will give me your word that, provided the information is of sufficient worth—and it is—you will instruct Medelli to open business corridors to my fledgling operation."

Guillermo nodded imperceptibly.

"Good," said Hawker. He lowered his voice as if what he was about to say required secrecy. "You've been infiltrated," he said. "You seem to know something of my own background, so you can understand that I still have friends in a position to . . . find out certain things. The informant is the local police chief, a man named Simps—"

"Simps!" snorted Guillermo. "He is just another cowardly, overweight American—"

"Wait until I finish. You're right; Simps is a coward. But he got caught taking payoffs as a cop in Miami. My people—" Hawker let himself smile, as if his tongue had slipped. "I mean, the people I once worked for brought the charges up again, to use

146

as leverage. They have Simps on a string. I don't expect you to believe me, so I will offer you some proof. I know that Simps was recently ordered to plant listening and tracking devices either on Medelli's boat or in the main house at Chatham Harbor."

"Where?" hissed Guillermo.

Hawker shrugged. "I'm not sure. From my own experience, I know that bathrooms are a favorite place—because that's often where people go to hold their most private talks. They think they're safe there."

Guillermo nodded and wiped the sweat from his face. He looked at his watch. "Mr. Thornton, you look as if you need a break from this Turkish torture. Why don't you go for a nice swim, and I will meet you back here in, say, fifteen minutes?"

Hawker watched the doughy man leave, then found the pool. The water wasn't as cold as he'd hoped it would be, and it stank of chlorine.

He swam a strong four hundred yards, working out the feeling of sloth that travel always produced in him, working out the tension of his careful lies to the South American diplomat.

Guillermo was already waiting when Hawker returned to the steam room.

"You checked?"

The South American nodded. "They found two of the devices. On the boat. One under the vanity and one in the main salon."

"There should be more. I know how they operate."

"Mr. Simps will be killed, of course. They are looking for him now. It seems he left town. But he will be back, and when he returns he will spend a very long time dying. In the end he will

beg them to allow him to die. Remember that, Mr. Thornton."
Guillermo's eyes were like stones. "The ultimate goals of my
organization need not concern you. You are a selfish man and
probably would not care anyway—and I do not mean that as an
insult. I already admire what little I know of you. Your record
seems to indicate that you have perceived what those of us from
other parts of the world have long known: America has grown
as weak and lazy and stupid as its citizenry. When the final fall
comes, there are those who are already prepared to take over."
He nodded as if in benediction. "But we will be the best prepared. And, more important, we will be first." He smiled. "Does
such a thing bother you?"

"I welcome the day," Hawker said airily.

"Good. Then I think it is possible that we can do business,
Mr. Thornton. But remember—many people have tried to take
advantage of us. And many, many people have died. Do I make
myself plain?"

"Spare me the threats, Mr. Guillermo. You're right: I am
a selfish man. I am so selfish that I always bargain fairly and
always hold up my end of a deal—because I know that in this
business you pay with your life if you don't." Hawker put just the
right edge in his voice, returning the threat.

"Good," said Guillermo with a laugh. "I would much prefer
we remain friends, for I fear you would be a difficult adversary."
He rubbed his hands together as if about to eat. "You have come
a long way, my new friend. Let us hear your business."

"It's probably small on your scale of operation. But, as I said,
we are just getting started. I can promise the future will hold
bigger and better things for both of us."

"I quite understand. And what is it you offer?"

"Cocaine. Forty pounds of it, uncut, eighty to ninety percent pure. A friend of mine from the organization was an operative in South America, and we are setting up a coca plantation, using two bogus missionaries to front for us. I've spent years studying the cocaine trade, and I think I've finally found a way to transport it in complete safety from South America to this country."

"And how is that?"

Hawker shook his head. "Perhaps I will tell you later—if our business dealings together are satisfactory. The forty pounds of cocaine was only an experimental shipment. We wanted to make sure my method would work. It did. Flawlessly."

"But only for small amounts, I suppose. Really, forty pounds is hardly worth the danger—"

"We can move as much as half a ton at a time using my method."

"Then why didn't you, Mr. Thornton?"

Hawker smiled. "As I said, the operation was experimental. I've now proved that it works." His smile broadened. "Plus we lacked working capital. We still do. That's why I've come to you."

"Again you intrigue me, Mr. Thornton. Of course, we have our own sources of cocaine. But if you will agree to share your method—"

"If our dealings are equitable, I will quite willingly sell it, Mr. Guillermo. No one with any brains deals in drugs for long. The odds catch up with you. I admire your very wise decision to stay safely on the outskirts. Personally, I plan to move out of this country within a year. But now I have forty pounds of cocaine for sale. Interested?"

"More in your technique than in the drug itself."

Which was exactly why Hawker had invented his imaginary fail-safe technique.

"I'll take that as a yes," said Hawker. "Here's my offer: The street value of cocaine, heavily cut, is about ninety thousand dollars a pound. Forty pounds is worth close to two million dollars."

"Which, of course, no one in the business would ever pay."

"Of course. The common wholesale price would be about eight hundred thousand. But since this is our first negotiation, as a sign of good faith, I would be willing to sell it to you for half that price."

"Four hundred thousand? Very fair," said Guillermo. "Too fair. What is the catch?"

"I want the money in foreign currency. Preferably in Venezuelan, since that is the most stable of your countries, but Colombian currency if need be. My reasons should be obvious. I can't account for large sums of money in this country as easily as you. Also, I want to make the exchange tonight. At two A.M., off an island called White Horse Key. Your people will know of it. I will be with two other men. We will be in a forty-foot fishing boat, the *Castaway*. We'll be anchored. Tell them not to attempt radio contact. Tell them to anchor Medelli's boat off Panther Key. Do you have that? It's important: Panther Key. Tell them to send one or two launches, without lights. They may send as many men as they want."

Guillermo nodded. "It is all very clear. But we would be willing to pay you twice as much money in U.S. currency."

"Absolutely not. I'm selfish, remember? I have no interest in being traced."

"In Colombian currency, then. But I must make myself plain on this point: Your revolutionary method of transporting cocaine had better be revolutionary. Without the promise of that, I would never have made this deal."

"I understand exactly what you mean," Hawker said, enjoying, for the moment, his private joke.

Hawker stood and opened the door. "One more thing, Mr. Guillermo. Your people on Mahogany Key have been riding roughshod over the villagers, who are sick of it. In fact, they're planning to raid your stronghold. Tonight."

Guillermo looked interested. "Is this a bit of free information, Mr. Thornton?"

"I think you know better. Nothing will bring the feds in faster than a mass killing on some remote Florida island. Tell your men not to use firearms. Fight them, sure. But if Medelli's people use guns, we're both in trouble."

Guillermo shook his head. "I quite agree, Mr. Thornton. Oddly enough, I expressed that very same feeling to Mr. Medelli only recently. The time will come when we will kill a great many of your silly race. But for now, killing only brings trouble."

Hawker forced himself to remain expressionless. "One more thing, Mr. Guillermo," he said evenly. "Did you have two men following me in a black Chevy?"

"Following you? Certainly not."

Hawker wondered if he was lying. "Good," he said. "It saved you some bail money."

Two hours later Hawker was on a plane, headed for Florida.

EIGHTEEN

It was nearly six P.M. before he drove across the bridge onto Mahogany Key.

It was a silver winter dusk, and a balmy wind blew from Florida Bay over the Everglades.

The place was like a ghost town. The streetlights were on, like little yellow moons, and houses were dark. Hawker guessed they must have sent the women and children out of town. It was a good idea. Hawker hadn't thought of it. Boggs McKay obviously had.

The parking lot at the Tarpon Inn was jammed with cars and pickup trucks. Lights blazed in the windows, and he could see that the dining room was full. Hawker took the back entrance to his cottage. He didn't want the men to see him. Not yet. He didn't want there to be any doubt about who was leading the assault on the Colombians.

The men of Mahogany Key wouldn't be men again until they drove the invaders out—by themselves.

Hawker tossed his duffel on his bed, stripped off his jacket and tie and went to work at the computer. It took him half an hour with RUSTLED to get the biography of James H. Thornton out of the Washington, D.C., data banks.

That done, he walked down to the docks to make sure the marina's old forty-foot fishing boat, *Castaway*, had been readied.

The boat smelled of diesel fuel and fresh paint. The tanks had been topped off, as Hawker had instructed, and one of the crates from his cottage had been loaded. The little yellow Bonefisher, with the 140-horsepower Johnson, had been tethered behind.

Hawker was just finishing his inspection when Logan came walking across the dock, surprisingly quiet for a man his size.

He held a revolver in his hand. "Hey!"

Hawker jumped. When Logan saw who it was, he lowered the weapon and grinned. "Christ, I thought we were being sabotaged. It's about time you got back. McKay's just about ready to lead the guys to Chatham Harbor, so you'd better hurry."

"I'm not going. Not with the men, anyway. I'm going to take one of the skiffs and watch from the mangroves. I want to keep an eye on things."

"What about later?" Logan asked. "I got the boat rigged just like you told me. The masks and fins and stuff are in the forward locker. And last night after the meeting, I spent about an hour with Graeme, showing him how to operate that hand-held missile launcher, the Stinger. Holy shit, you brought enough stuff with you to outfit an army. Where'd you get it?"

Hawker stepped onto the dock and patted Logan on the back. "Never mind where I got it. I just want to be sure you know what you're getting into tonight. It's going to be rough. And bloody. Some people are going to die—maybe us."

Logan shook his head comically. "If I can survive three tours in Nam, this will be like going on a picnic. Honest to god, Hawk, sometimes the shit came down so heavy over there I used to wonder why they didn't issue us umbrellas."

"You're sure?"

"Damn right."

"Logan, I've had my suspicions that you might be a federal agent: FBI or—"

"Just a cook," said Logan. "I'm just a cook."

"I keep forgetting." Hawker held out his hand. "Anyway, I appreciate it. Good luck. And I'll see you at midnight."

Logan grinned. "Hope you enjoy the show. That Boggs McKay is something. One hell of a leader. I think the boys are going to kick some ass for a change." Logan had started down the dock but stopped suddenly, snapping his fingers. "Oh," he said. "I have a message for you."

"Yeah?"

"Yeah. Graeme took it. From some guy named . . . Schmidt. Said he was calling from Washington. Said it was important."

"What was the message?"

"All he said was, 'It's fake.' That was the whole message: 'It's fake.' Kind of strange, huh?"

Hawker's hands slowly became fists. "No," he said. "It's not strange. It's exactly what I expected."

Hawker returned to his cottage.

He pulled on camouflaged army duck commando pants and a black oiled wool sweater. He covered his red hair with a black wool watch cap. He used a charcoal stick on his face and hands.

Now he had some tough weaponry choices to make. He strapped on the Jensen quick-draw side holster and added his custom .45-caliber Commander. He had planted his Gerber Mark II knife on the Colombian, but he still had his best knife: a handmade Randall Attack/Survival, a masterpiece of steel.

He had three choices of field weaponry: the Remington 700, the Ingram submachine gun or a Colt Commando automatic rifle. Hawker decided on the Commando, which was really a shorter version of the M16. He knew most of the fighting would be in close, and the Colt's telescoping stock would be ideal. Also, the Star-Tron night vision scope could be mounted on it.

Hawker filled a half dozen of the twenty-round detachable box clips and shoved another into the weapon itself. Once the Star-Tron was fixed, he was ready.

Just before he left, he tried to call Winnie Tiger. He knew how stubborn she was, and he suspected she probably hadn't left town with the other women.

There was no answer.

Hawker was glad. As tough as the Indian beauty was, even she wouldn't want to be around tonight.

Hawker climbed into the little rowboat and pulled himself across the dark bay.

Night herons squawked from the mangrove shadows, and stars glimmered above.

There was a light wind out of the northwest, and the occasional flare of distant lightning illuminated sea clouds on the horizon. A storm was rolling toward them from the Gulf of Mexico, and Hawker was glad. The cover and noise of a rough sea would help.

At the edge of Chatham Harbor, Hawker steered the skiff into the mangroves and tied it against the tidal stream. Lights were on in the dozen houses at the edge of the harbor, but no music blared, and no men drank beer on the porches. A nervous silence seemed to hang over the settlement.

The warehouse was about fifty yards away, off to the right. The same two guards stood in the white lights of the dock. They didn't look bored now. They were alert, smoking nervously. They kept their rifles close. Hawker knew that Guillermo had warned them. He studied them through the Star-Tron scope, seeing their faces clearly. The Colt Commando had an effective range of two hundred meters. It was more than enough.

If they didn't follow orders, if they opened fire on the men of Mahogany Key, Hawker would kill them. There would be no waiting for orders from stupid little politicians on this night.

The *Demonio Del Mar*, Medelli's hundred-foot yacht, was gone. Hawker was surprised. He had gotten the impression that Guillermo would have them keep the yacht safely at dockside until it was near the 2 A.M. rendezvous time. It worried him. What if Medelli had decided to double-cross Guillermo and strike out on his own? What if Hawker's warning to Guillermo was leading the local fishermen into an ambush?

Hawker tightened his grip on the Colt Commando and waited.

Finally he saw them through the Star-Tron: Boggs McKay leading the initial strike force through the bushes. Boggs carried the explosives in a backpack. It took Hawker a moment to recognize the stocky, bullnecked older man behind him: Buck Hamilton, the real owner of the Tarpon Inn.

Hamilton had made good on his promise. He had returned to Mahogany Key in time to fight the Colombians again.

It was a simple plan. Boggs and his men would hit them straight on. When the Colombians rallied and the fighting began, two other groups, led by Mellor and Logan, would hit them from each flank.

Even though most of the men carried handguns, both McKay and Hawker had agreed they should not fire unless their lives were in danger. They wanted to help them win back their self-respect, not turn them into killers. As Hawker well knew, for every human life you take, you die a little bit yourself. And these men had already suffered enough.

As McKay led his men onward, Hawker could see the patrol of Colombians heading toward them. There were about twenty of them, carrying clubs as heavy as ax handles.

Hawker wanted to shout out a warning. He didn't. It was up to the fishermen now. They would have to win or lose on their own. Hawker waved some mosquitoes away from his face and did nothing.

McKay saw the Colombians before the others. He gave his men a hand signal, telling them to spread out. Then, with a rebel war whoop, he charged right at the Colombians. His men charged right behind.

Hawker had been afraid for the fishermen. His fears were soon put to rest. They fought like demons. With the initial charge, the rest of the Colombians poured out of their houses, swarming toward Boggs McKay's men.

The fishermen met them with their heads high, fists swinging. It was then that Logan's men attacked the Colombians from the bushes on the left flank, and Graeme Mellor's men hit them from the right.

They had the Colombians in the middle now. The fishermen were slightly outnumbered, and the Colombians seemed to have youth and strength on their side.

But it didn't matter. The fishermen fought as a team now. They fought for their homes, for their women, for their young sons and daughters. Hawker had never seen anything like it. One of the fishermen, just out of his teens, got hit from the side with one of the clubs. He turned, grinning through his bloody face, then jerked the club from the Colombian's hands and beat him to the ground with it.

From the cluster of houses around the harbor, someone fired off a parachute flare, as if light might help the Colombians. For a wild minute the whole battleground was illuminated in the ghastly red glow. For the Colombians it was like hell. For the fishermen it was like the Fourth of July.

They were winning their independence; they were retaking their homeland.

Buck Hamilton had improvised an interesting method of attack. Because he was older and fatter than most of the other fishermen, the Colombians thought him an easy mark. Buck had wisely decided to use that to his advantage. He spent most of his time down on his hands and knees, crawling around on the grass. When a Colombian would trot up to give the final death blow, Buck would crack him in the shins with an ax handle, then all but decapitate the man as he bent over in pain. Hawker counted at least four men he'd put out that way.

Boggs McKay, Graeme Mellor and Logan were proving themselves equally tough.

Logan had found himself a good place to stand and fight: at the edge of the seawall, with a car at his back. The Colombians had to come at him head on, which was just what Logan wanted. One by one he would slap their clubs away with his left forearm, then pop their faces open with his sledge-size right fist. When they hit the ground, he would scoop them up in his bearish arms and toss them into the bay.

Hawker thought Logan had had it once. A towering black man made it through his defense and succeeded in getting around behind him and getting his club stretched across Logan's throat. He was being choked to death. Hawker was just about to jump out of the skiff when Logan jammed his elbow into the black man's ribs, spun, butted his face bloody, then added another body to the bay.

Graeme Mellor did his fighting at the base of a huge oak tree. He had obviously had a lot of karate training. He used spinning kicks and elbow blows to send his attackers unconscious to the ground.

Rather than standing and fighting, Boggs McKay roamed the grounds like a monster man. Whenever the Colombians began to gang up on a fallen fisherman, Boggs was there, his big fists working like hammers.

The Colombians were taking one hell of a beating. They began to fall back toward the houses, slowly at first, then in a mass panic.

The fishermen went right after them. Through the Star-Tron

scope, Hawker could see Buck Hamilton leading the way. His nose was bloody, and he was grinning as he jogged after the Colombians. Every time one came within range, Buck hurried him on his way with a swift kick in the ass.

As he ran Hamilton began to dig something out of his shirt. Hawker finally realized what it was: a flag. An American flag. There was an empty flagpole in one of the yards, and Buck found it. He snapped the flag to the halyard and began to raise it. When it was halfway up, Hamilton's knees suddenly buckled and he grabbed his chest.

For a moment Hawker thought he was having a heart attack. But then he heard the compressed *thud* of the second shot and realized the Colombians had opened fire.

Hamilton's knees buckled again. He shook his head defiantly, and with tremendous willpower, he pulled the flag high and snubbed the rope to the cleat before collapsing to the grass.

It was no longer just a fight. It was a war.

Hawker's head swung, and he saw that it was the guards at the warehouse who were firing. Each man's rifle had a round, tubular silencer. Hawker switched the Colt Commando to automatic fire and swept the dock with a long burst. The two men jolted as if they had just touched a high-voltage line, and they fell kicking and screaming to the cement quay.

There was the sound of more fire now, automatic weapons fire. It was coming from the main house. It had the fishermen pinned down. Worse, they were sitting ducks. A couple of them fired back with their handguns, but with little effect.

Hawker waded to shore. He made his way through the bushes toward the house. There was a stretch of open yard, and he sprinted, drawing fire. He dove, rolled and came to his feet safely under the house. He dropped the Commando's spent clip and jammed a fresh one in.

He knew they'd be watching for him at the doors of the house. He slung the rifle over his shoulder and jumped up and grabbed the porch beam. He pulled himself up and slid under the railing onto the porch. With his back against the wall, Hawker peeked into the window.

There were three men in the room, all carrying strange-looking automatic rifles. Hawker finally recognized them: AK-47s, Soviet assault rifles.

If the Mahogany Key puzzle needed a final piece to be complete, this was it.

Anton Nuñez Guillermo wasn't kidding when he said his people would be ready for America's final fall. His organization obviously had a very powerful friend: the USSR.

The men stood at three different parts of the room, all watching a door. Hawker needed to get them all looking in the same direction. There was a potted plant on the porch near his feet: an aloe plant, good for healing burns. Hawker lifted it and gave it a high, arching toss toward the far door. The moment their heads swung, Hawker put his head down and rolled through the screen.

He came to his feet, spraying the Colombians with 5.56-millimeter slugs, slamming two of them dead against the wall and knocking the third out the door. The Colombian gave a final death scream before he hit the ground.

When he was sure the house was empty, Hawker went out onto the porch and waved the fishermen onward. They came charging out of the bushes, ready for more. But this time they wanted blood. Buck Hamilton was well liked on the island, and the fishermen wanted revenge.

The Colombians sensed it. They ran for their lives. Some of them dove into the bay. Others jammed into cars and sped away.

Hawker went down the wooden steps three at a time and sprinted to the flagpole where Buck lay. Boggs McKay, Logan and Mellor were already there, all kneeling over him.

"Is he dead?" Hawker asked anxiously.

And a testy old voice answered, "Shit, no, I ain't dead, you ol' coconut-headed boy. Them slimy devils just put a couple of leak holes in me."

Hawker laughed at the sight before him. Buck Hamilton rested supine on the grass, his head propped, a crooked smile on his face. Logan was applying direct pressure to his shoulder while Mellor worked on his leg.

"Goddamn if we didn't pull it off, Hawk!" crowed Hamilton. "Hey, hey! All you boys gather 'round here. I got an announcement to make!"

Forty or more fishermen closed in to listen. They were sweaty and bleeding, but they were happy; to a man, they were grinning triumphantly.

"I got a couple of things to say before I let these boys cart me off to the hospital in Naples," Hamilton continued, breathing heavily and obviously in pain. "First off, this ugly redheaded man standing beside me here, James Hawker, deserves a hell of a lot of thanks from all of us. Christ, when I left seven weeks ago, this island looked like a goddamn ghost town. Now it looks like a model city—my own Tarpon Inn included!"

The fishermen cheered and slapped Hawker on the back. Hawker didn't embarrass easily, but he was embarrassed now.

"And I got one more thing to say!" bellowed Buck Hamilton. He gave it just the right pause before adding, "Drinks are on the house!"

Hooting and bragging and joking, the fishermen headed off through the darkness back to the Tarpon Inn and their celebration party.

Hawker held out his hand to Boggs McKay. McKay's rugged face looked strangely at peace. "You're a hell of a leader," said Hawker as the two big men shook hands. "Those men couldn't have done it without you."

"Or you," said McKay, a wry smile on his face. "It's not often I let myself be used, but this time . . . well, this time I was the one who benefited. Thanks, Hawker. I mean that. Another year as a hermit and I don't think I would ever have recovered."

"Welcome back to the living, breathing world, Boggs. And if you decide you want to go back into business, or maybe even politics—"

"I think I can handle it from here," McKay said with a laugh. "The offer is appreciated, though."

Hawker nodded. "Good luck."

After promising Buck Hamilton he would visit him in the hospital, Hawker took Logan and Mellor aside. "Do you fellows still want to go with me tonight? If you're not up to it, just say—"

"Have you noticed how I keep looking at my watch?" interrupted Logan.

"Your watch? Well, er, no—"

"Do you remember those explosives you gave Boggs to carry?" asked Mellor innocently.

"Right," said Hawker. "I remember—"

"The warehouse is set to go off in four minutes and fifty-five seconds. . . . No, make that fifty-three seconds. . . . No, make that—"

"Boggs!" Hawker yelled. "Get Buck ready to move out or we'll all be joining him in the hospital! I'm beginning to think this goddamn cook of ours really is just a cook!"

When they were halfway down Bayside Drive, they turned and watched. Graeme did the countdown. "Fifteen, fourteen, thirteen . . ."

The warehouse erupted in a gush of orange light that shook the earth, illuminated the harbor and rained fire down on the bay.

From behind them at the Tarpon Inn, they could hear the fishermen cheering.

Hawker was not surprised at what spun down from the sky, floating soft as snowflakes.

It was money.

NINETEEN

Just after midnight Hawker, Logan and Mellor got aboard the *Castaway* and idled from the dock into the mangrove darkness of the bay.

The wind had freshened, coming cold out of the northwest, and lightning glowed in distant storm clouds over the Gulf.

The cruiser punched through the heavy chop of Chatham Bay, wallowing in the troughs of waves, cavitating, then dieseling onward through the blackness.

Behind them, the Colombians' warehouse still burned, and the party at the Tarpon Inn continued. An ambulance had come for Buck Hamilton. As he was lifted onto the stretcher, he had waved jauntily and asked for a dip of snuff.

Logan had been out enough with Harley Bates, the fishing guide, to know the water. He steered. Mellor sat beside him with the chart. They ran without lights, and it was up to Mellor to count the points of islands so they would not get lost in the jungled maze.

Hawker stood uneasily on the stern deck, going over their

equipment and gauging the strength of the coming squall. It looked like they were in for some very foul weather indeed.

Hawker nodded, approving. It was good. The noise would provide them with cover.

Logan wound the boat through the treacherous backcountry. Twice the cruiser jolted, churning mud in the shallow water. Mangrove limbs scraped past the wheelhouse in the narrow channels. The deck was littered with limbs and branches.

Finally they broke into a star-glazed river of deep water. It was Dismal Key Pass. Logan took a deep breath and rolled his shoulder muscles, trying to relieve the tension of the difficult steering.

"This is it," he said. "Graeme, you can take the boat into the Gulf from here. Just keep her right in the middle of the channel." He looked at Hawker and smiled. "This is it, boss. Time to go it alone."

"Let's get the gear into the Bonefisher." Hawker gave Graeme Mellor a light slap on the back. "Don't forget—don't let Medelli's men get too close. And don't let them get a clear shot at you—they might take it. Use the bullhorn to communicate. Tell them to tie the money to a life jacket and set it adrift. Make them hold it up in the light first. Make sure it's Venezuelan or Colombian. You do the same with that plastic bag of baking soda. Throw it as far as you can. Once they get it, tell them to get the hell away. We should be ready by that time. And if they give you any trouble at all, lob a grenade at them. Or, if they're far enough away, use the Stinger. Got it?"

Mellor wiped his hand across his lips. He grinned. "My mouth's too bloody dry to talk."

"Don't worry. If things go like I plan, we'll pull it off without a shot being fired. They think you're on their side, remember?"

As Graeme Mellor steered the *Castaway* toward the open Gulf for his rendezvous at White Horse Key, Logan and Hawker got the skiff on plane. The 140-horsepower Johnson blew the Bonefisher across the water as if it were a jet boat.

The wind blew hard over the bay, and they jumped the waves with jarring impact, taking spray over the bow.

One by one openings in the islands revealed themselves as Logan whipped the skiff through the narrow cut at Four Brothers Key and into the bay below Hog Key.

Ahead, the flour-colored beach of Panther Key looked gray in the darkness. There was a sudden explosion of lightning, like a flashbulb going off, and for a moment Hawker could see the black outline of *Demonio Del Mar* anchored on the far Gulf side of the island.

Logan pulled the skiff into a little harbor protected by mangroves, using the trim button to raise the engine as they grounded ashore.

Wordlessly the two men readied themselves. Hawker tied off the skiff while Logan unloaded their gear. They slung packs and weaponry over their shoulders and headed along the tree line at a heavy jog.

At the coral shoals of Gomez Point, waves pounded over the reef. Hawker pulled off his running shoes and adjusted the black Rocket fins.

"Looks like a good night for a swim," he chided Logan.

"Shit, why can't we just use that rocket launcher and blow up the boat from here? It's as rough as a damn cob out on that sea."

"Because I have a hunch there's something very important on board, something we can't risk looking for ever again."

Logan was uncomfortably quiet for a moment. "What about sharks?" he finally blurted.

Hawker looked at him, incredulous. "What the hell do you mean, sharks?"

"You know goddamn well what I mean—those big ugly bastards with fins and teeth."

"You did three tours on Nam and you're worried about *fish?*" Hawker burst out laughing.

"They didn't have fucking sharks in Quang Tri!" Logan yelled in a whisper. He snorted in disgust. "You don't get out enough, Hawker. You need to start seeing some movies; no shit. If there's a white shark within two miles of here, we might as well kiss our asses good-bye, because those bastards are *bad*. Must have noses like fucking bloodhounds—"

"For God's sake, Logan, don't worry." Hawker spat in his mask, rinsed it, then backed into the surf. "The Colombians are probably going to kill us anyway."

"Thanks!" Logan called after him.

"It's just that it's hard to believe an FBI agent is afraid of a fish."

"I don't work for the damn government!" Logan yelled as Hawker disappeared into the surf. "When are you going to get that through your thick skull! I'm just a—" Logan didn't finish. Hawker had already disappeared into the water. Logan pulled the mask down over his shaggy hair. Mumbling to himself, he followed Hawker into the night sea.

It was a mile swim through windswept waves and a strong southerly tide.

When they were less than two hundred yards away, Hawker

saw the deck lights of *Demonio Del Mar* flare briefly as one of the Whalers was lowered.

Hawker had hoped they would send both boats. The fewer people to deal with on the yacht, the better off he would be. He sculled water and watched them load the skiff with men and weapons. The engine fired, and the Whaler, carrying four men, pounded off toward White Horse Key and the rendezvous with Graeme Mellor on the *Castaway*.

Silently Hawker wished his friend luck. But he had a feeling Logan and he would need even more luck.

The yacht was a black mountain before them now, lifting and rolling on its ground tackle. The two men grabbed the anchor chain and rested there, lifting, rising and falling with the sea.

"How do you feel?" Hawker asked in a whisper.

"Great. The damn sharks had me worried. I've got it made now, though." Logan's mask was propped on his forehead, and he was smiling.

"Good. Swing around and let me get the stuff out of your pack."

Hawker removed four time-detonated incendiary bombs. They had magnetic bases and would latch easily to the steel hull of *Demonio Del Mar*. The sheet bodies of the bombs were filled with fifteen hundred grams of thermate, a composition that burns for nearly two minutes at 2150 degrees. Thermate can burn through a solid inch of armor plating. Hawker knew the bombs would sear through the hull of the yacht as though it were butter.

"You get these mounted under the bow area. I'll take the other two and mount one amidships and the other toward the stern." Hawker studied the soft green glow of his watch. "We'll give ourselves . . . sixty minutes." The bombs had timer switches, and the men ground the dials almost a full turn clockwise. "Start . . . *now.*"

Hawker let the current carry him toward the back of the boat. He pulled his mask down and dove. It was like diving into ink. He had to do everything by feel. The bottom of the boat was slick with moss. There was the glass-shard edge of barnacles. Hawker caught hold of the starboard drive shaft and clamped one of the bombs forward of it, under the engines. He surfaced, took two deep bites of air and locked the second incendiary bomb under the wide stern section.

It was 2:11 A.M.

He kicked himself forward to the bow. Logan was waiting. "We've got to get up that anchor chain—and we've got to make it quick and quiet. I'll go first. For all I know, a guard will be looking right at me as I pull myself onto the deck. If you hear any firing, get the hell back to Panther Key—quick. You got it?"

Logan nodded. "Are you sure this little submachine gun will still fire after the soaking it took?" He motioned with his head toward the Ingram strapped to his shoulder.

"Anybody's guess," said Hawker as he began to pull himself up the anchor chain.

"Comforting," said Logan. "Very comforting."

The chain was slick, and the links cut into his hands, but Hawker finally made it to the top. He grabbed hold of the pulpit railing and hauled himself over the bowsprit onto the deck.

He unslung the Colt Commando automatic and lay on his belly. Directly in front of him was a heavy mound of canvas:

probably emergency anchors and line. Hawker slid in tighter behind its cover and waited.

Soon Logan came huffing over the bow, dripping water. He collapsed belly-first beside Hawker.

"Son of a bitch," he gasped. "I haven't worked that hard since Special Forces training."

Hawker held up a finger for silence. As he had expected, there were guards on the deck. From around the port walkway, a figure in a dark coat was coming toward them. The guard approached warily, like a field dog that sees a snake.

Hawker cupped a hand around Logan's ear. "Don't fire unless you absolutely have to."

Logan nodded.

From the ankle sheath Hawker drew the Randall Attack/Survival knife. The blade was seven inches of hand-finished steel, honed like a razor on both sides.

The guard was coming closer. He had heard them. The weapon in his hands was either a rifle or a shotgun. In the darkness Hawker couldn't tell for sure.

Five paces away the guard stopped. He studied the mound of canvas curiously. He reached out with the long gun, as if to move the canvas. Quicker than Hawker thought was possible, Logan grabbed the barrel of the gun, jerking it away. Hawker was already in motion. He caught the guard by the hair, spun him and plunged the knife through the soft underjaw area into the man's head.

The guard trembled in Hawker's arms, like a dying fish, before collapsing to the deck. The corpse made odd gurgling noises.

"One down," whispered Logan.

Crouched and ready, the two men moved across the fore-deck toward the wheelhouse. The wind was churning harder now, and the yacht heaved and yawed. A sharp rain began to fall, blown into a flat, bulletlike trajectory by the wind.

Inside the wheelhouse was the sudden flame of a lighter as two men fired their cigarettes. Hawker waved Logan in behind him.

"If we can," he whispered, "we'll tie them and gag them."

They never got the chance to try. Just as they got to the hatchway, lightning exploded, illuminating the deck in a searing light.

Hawker saw the men's eyes widen in understanding as they each jumped for their automatic rifles. Hawker swung through the doorway as Logan's Ingram chain-rattled in a twenty-round burst. The Colombians slammed against the steel bulkhead, dying—but not before one of them pulled some kind of alarm.

There was a loud siren wail, whipped away by the storm wind.

Lights flashed on. Men poured from below decks like ants from a damaged hill. There was shouting in garbled Spanish.

"We are in for some shit now!" Logan whispered hoarsely.

Hawker didn't have time to answer. Something ricocheted past his head. Slugs traced their way along the deck from two sides. Hawker dove from the wheelhouse, rolled and came to one knee, the Colt Commando thudding against his shoulder.

One Colombian screamed and grabbed his face. Another Colombian was kicked backward over the railing into the green sweep of sea.

Logan had taken the port side. His submachine gun spewed fire, and three more Colombians fell.

From above them on the fly bridge, Hawker heard the sound of running feet. He pulled himself up the ladder, then ducked as a .357 slug peeled the paint away above him. He locked his arm around the ladder, popped in a fresh ammo clip, then jumped to his feet, spraying the fly bridge.

The man with the revolver stumbled backward, spinning. A flare of lightning showed that his white uniform was dotted with red. He clutched desperately at a canvas sun shield. The canvas ripped away as he plummeted ten feet through the wheelhouse's slanted windows.

From the top deck Hawker had a fair view of the entire deck. A dozen or more Colombians had taken cover behind the raised aft cabin. They had Logan pinned down with heavy automatic weapons fire. The occasional clatter of the little Ingram told Hawker that Logan was still alive.

Because of the swim they had to make, Hawker had removed the Star-Tron scope. But the Commando wasn't noted for its accuracy anyway; the barrel was too short for any kind of sharp-shooting.

In the olive drab pack he wore, Hawker found one of the M34 incendiary/fragmentation hand grenades. The serrated steel body was heavy in his right hand. The grenade was filled with 425 grams of white phosphorus that would burn at 2700 degrees for a full minute. Hawker would have four to five seconds after pulling the pin before the grenade exploded, and the fragmentation kill radius was as much as thirty meters.

"Stay low!" he yelled down to Logan.

"Do I have a fucking choice? Those bastards have me covered like stink on shit!"

"Not for much longer!"

Hawker jerked the pin out, counted a quick three, then lofted the grenade overhand toward the aft cabin. The M34 exploded just before it hit, showering the deck with blinding white light.

The screams were terrible to hear. The Colombians not on fire dove headlong into the stormy sea. The stern of the vessel was encased in a roaring chemical fire.

Hawker swung down to the main deck. Logan was waiting, the Ingram balanced on his hip, covering him.

"Let's make this quick," Hawker shouted.

Shielding their faces from the intense heat, Hawker and Logan made their way along the outside of the trunk cabin, then swung into the safety of the below-decks passageway. There they rested for a moment, catching their wind.

"I hope whatever it is you're after is worth all this shit," Logan said and snorted, half laughing. He took a soaked plug of Red Man from its green foil pack and bit off a wad. "Chew?"

"I gave it up when I stopped playing baseball." Hawker reconsidered and took the plug, adding, "But I just decided to start again."

The two men spat, grinning.

"What the hell are we after, anyway?"

"You'll see," Hawker said. "If we can find it."

They kicked open doors one by one and flipped on lights, moving down the passageway. Forward of the engines, the passageway formed a T. Halfway there, two Colombians in khaki military dress jumped out. Hawker and Logan dropped to their bellies simultaneously, firing. One Hispanic fell to the deck, his face blown away. The other crumpled to his knees, fumbling for something in his pocket. Hawker watched the grenade arching toward them as if in slow motion.

Logan dove for an open door. Hawker dove for the grenade. In one motion he caught it, cocked his arm from hip level and drilled it back at the guard.

The explosion rattled the boat and showered them with paint, dust and flesh.

"You must have been a hell of a baseball player," Logan whispered, sticking his head up.

"No," said Hawker absently. A room at the end of the hall had caught his attention. "If I'd been any good, I'd be in the majors right now." He stood and studied the door. A sign read: AIR STATION, NO ADMITTANCE. He tapped Logan with a back of his hand. "Hey, this might be what we're looking for."

Side by side they approached the door. Hawker stopped for a moment and checked his watch. It was 2:30 A.M.

They didn't have much time: only thirty-odd minutes. At Hawker's nod, they kicked the door open and jumped into the room, weapons vectoring; ready.

Hawker was stunned.

The huge mulatto, Simio, stood near a stack of aluminum scuba tanks, glowering at them.

Medelli lay dead on the floor, blood pooling from the bullethole in his head.

In the far corner of the room was a generator attached to a complex series of rollers and colored tubes. Anton Nuñez Guillermo, his St. Nicholas face flushed, stood beside the press, a 9-millimeter parabellum in his right hand.

"It seems I have underestimated you, Mr. James Thornton

Hawker," he hissed. "But I assure you it will be the very last time. Now drop your weapons, gentlemen. Drop them and kick them away."

Slowly, then, he raised the automatic and pressed the barrel against the head of the woman in the chair beside him.

Dr. Winnie Tiger looked at Hawker briefly, then turned her eyes away.

TWENTY

"I see you two know each other," Guillermo said with a smile, releasing his grip on the Indian woman.

Hawker tried to catch her eye. He hoped she would give him some signal, some expression, to let him know she was all right. But she kept her head down, hands clamped tightly together.

Guillermo moved a few steps closer to Hawker and Logan. He motioned to the corpse of Medelli on the deck. "This has been a troublesome week for my organization," he said. "First, my operatives told me that Mr. Medelli had been cheating me. But worse—much, much worse—I was told that he had decided to try and take over *my* organization."

Guillermo studied Hawker with cold brown eyes. "And then you came to my very door, Mr. Hawker. A clever fellow. A very clever fellow." He chuckled softly. "I must admit that I fell for your little story. But I am a careful man, Mr. Hawker. I decided to check out your background through other sources. Fortunately one of my people on Mahogany Key had been keeping an eye on you. A close eye." He shrugged. "And so I decided such a delicate situation required my personal attention." He motioned toward the corpse again. "I've already taken care of Mr. Medelli. Now it is your turn, Mr. Hawker. It is time for you and your burly friend to die."

Hawker tried to keep his voice flat and businesslike. "I can understand why you have to kill me. I know all about your operation, Guillermo, and I know that running drugs is just part of it. A very small part of it. I don't know how you got Winnie. I suppose one of your people told you that we were romantically involved, and you decided she would be an ideal bargaining tool. Well, they were right. I'm willing to bargain—but only if you release Winnie and my friend here. They know nothing about your real operation—"

Guillermo threw his head back and laughed loudly. "Bargain? With you? Really, Mr. Hawker, your spirit is admirable but, in this case, quite silly. You are in my power—"

"I have a detailed report of your operation in a safety deposit box, and I left directions with a friend to open it if I don't return—"

"*Enough!*" Guillermo's face was pallid with anger. "I've heard enough of your insulting stories!" He visibly calmed himself. "You and your party are going to die, Mr. Hawker. Medelli had been with me for some time, so I allowed him to die painlessly. But I owe you no such favors. Would you like to see how you are going to die?" Guillermo's smile was a thin, dark slit. He motioned toward the mulatto giant. "Simio, dispose of their weapons, please."

The mulatto rumbled across the deck. First he picked up the Ingram. He put one fist around the metal stock and the other around the silencer. Holding it away from his body, he began to bend it. The sweat beaded on his forehead, and his knuckles turned white.

The submachine gun twisted as if it were rubber.

He tossed it aside and crumpled the Colt Commando in the same fashion.

"That is how you are going to die, Mr. Hawker." Guillermo chuckled. "He will start with your arms. And then he will turn his attention—and his considerable strength—to your legs. You have been a great deal of trouble, and you will not be allowed to die easily. In the end you will beg. Have you ever heard a man begging to be killed? I have—but not so often as the incomparable Simio. You see, gentlemen, Simio enjoys such things. It is how we reward him. See how his eyes now glisten? See how he moves his tongue over his lips, like a hungry cat before it toys with the mouse?" When Hawker did not react, the Colombian diplomat snorted. "Kill them one at a time, Simio. Mr. Hawker first, please. And take your time."

The mulatto grinned through ragged teeth. He came at Hawker, legs bent in a crouch, hands held high and loose like a wrestler.

Hawker squared himself, left foot slightly forward, left fist at chest level, right fist low and ready.

When Simio was within distance, Hawker faked a quick left, then buried his right fist in the giant's throat. The mulatto was caught off guard and backpedaled across the room and crashed into the stack of scuba tanks. They rolled and clattered across the floor.

"Hawk, watch it!"

From the corner of his eye he saw Guillermo leveling the parabellum at him. Logan moved first, diving toward the diplomat. He hit him thigh high, and hard—but not hard enough.

Guillermo clubbed Logan viciously on the head with the gun, then got off one quick shot.

Hawker saw blood and flesh explode from Logan's back, but somehow the big vet got a fist on the weapon and turned it slowly, slowly toward the Colombian.

There was the *ker-wack* of a shot, but Hawker didn't see the rest. There was a sudden, bone-creaking impact, and he was being driven across the room.

There was a blinding white light, and the ammonia scent of unconsciousness as he was powered onward toward the steel bulkhead—and death.

In the last moment some clarity of thought—instinct, perhaps, from his years of boxing and baseball—told him what to do. He let his knees collapse, and the mulatto plowed over him, colliding face first with the wall.

There was a high-pitched ripping sound, and for a moment Hawker thought it was his own back muscles tearing.

He looked up. Simio was shaking his bloody face, dazed. It would have been funny if the situation hadn't been so deadly—his pants had ripped open on impact, exposing the bulging, dark buttocks.

The mulatto bellowed in rage and came at Hawker, the heavy fists swinging.

He managed to catch the first few punches on his arms and shoulders. It felt as if every punch crushed bone. Then a glancing blow scraped the top of his head, and Hawker tumbled backward over the jumble of aluminum tanks.

He pulled himself shakily to his knees, his back to Simio. He knew he had only one chance to stun the man. He also knew he had to time it perfectly.

He did.

Just as the mulatto reached for him, Hawker swung around hard and caught Simio flush on the ear with his elbow. But the giant did not go down. Hawker began throwing punches at his throat, one after another just like on the heavy bag back in the Bridgeport gym, head low, eyes up, swinging hard with wrists snapping so the knuckles cut like knives, driving with rhythm from the hips, hitting through his target.

The mulatto stopped some of the punches, but not all of them. Hawker was backing him up, seeing the brown face glisten and grow pale, seeing the albino-blue eyes bulge, seeing the giant's anger turn to pure hatred, and he knew this fight would be to the death.

Simio stumbled finally and fell face first to the floor. There was a knife in a sheath on his belt, and Hawker saw the massive right hand feel for it.

With the last of his strength, Hawker grabbed one of the aluminum scuba tanks in both hands and held it overhead, thinking to knock the mulatto unconscious.

But then he had another idea. He pointed the valve at Simio's exposed buttocks, harpooned the tank downward and—because the man beneath him was one of those sick, vicious creatures who injured and murdered for pleasure—Hawker turned the air valve full open.

There was a pressurized *sissssz*, a sudden bloating of the giant's body, then an internal explosion as the mulatto shuddered, dead.

Hawker turned dizzily. Logan lay bleeding on the floor. Guillermo had been shot in the chest, but he was moving . . . moving toward the parabellum that rested in the middle of the room. Winnie Tiger stood watching with hard, dark eyes.

"Winnie," Hawker said, his voice oddly raspy. "Get it. Get the gun."

His voice seemed to startle her. She looked at him quickly, then looked at the automatic. Her step was slow, then faster.

Guillermo was a foot away, reaching with outstretched hand, his burning eyes turned on Hawker.

"Winnie, get the damn gun!"

She grabbed it just before Guillermo did. She looked at the wounded Colombian on the floor, then looked at Hawker. Her face look pale and strange, as if in shock.

Slowly she raised the weapon over Guillermo's head . . .

"You don't have to kill him, Winnie. You don't have to do that—"

. . . leveling the parabellum, holding it in small hands, both eyes open and sighting professionally down the barrel . . .

"For Christ's sake, Winnie, back away from him. He's going to grab your legs—"

. . . her beautiful Indian face dull and dead, yet filled with a strange seething as she swung the automatic toward Hawker.

"You . . . you're the cause of all this!" she whispered, for once letting the Spanish accent seep into her voice. "Now I . . . I must . . . I must kill *you!*"

"*Hold it!*"

The door of the room jolted open, and Graeme Mellor stood holding a stub-nosed .38. Winnie Tiger jumped and shot off balance, and Mellor fired once, the slug tearing through the shoulder of the white blouse she wore, driving her backward over Guillermo.

Hawker looked at Mellor, stunned, hearing—yet not hearing—Mellor's voice as he kneeled over Winnie Tiger, touching her perfect face with trembling fingers. "She's Guillermo's daughter, Hawk. I wanted to tell you, but I couldn't. We've been monitoring the operation for the last six months. She was sent down here to keep an eye on Medelli. He knew it. That was why he tried to have her killed. I got to the Colombian who was supposed to do it, but not before Sandy Rand stumbled onto him."

Mellor kneeled quickly over Logan, then touched his index finger to Guillermo's neck and then Winnie Tiger's. "Guillermo's dead. Logan and the woman are both still alive, Hawk. We've got to get out of here."

For the first time Hawker thought of the incendiary bombs. He checked his watch. It was 2:47 A.M.

"We've got to get the plates!" Hawker commanded, already searching the room.

"Plates? What plates? What the hell are you talking about?"

Hawker found the fifty-dollar plate mounted in the printing press. The others were nearby, in a velvet-lined case of mahogany.

"These plates," Hawker said, holding one up. "The whole drug thing was a cover. They wanted to take over the country, Mellor, and they thought they'd found a way to do it: make their own money and then keep it out of wide circulation by investing it in properties and industry. They weren't getting rich running drugs. That's why no one ever caught them. They were counterfeiting money. Perfect money. Almost."

Quickly Hawker dropped the plates in his pack and reached for Winnie Tiger's wrist. Her eyes fluttered open, focused, and her soft lips moved as if to speak. Hawker drew closer.

"You . . . you," she whispered weakly. "I didn't want to kill you. I loved . . . I loved you, but I . . . but I . . ."

"Later," said James Hawker. "We can talk later. If you can just hold on for a while longer, we'll have all the time in the world to talk."

At 3:04 A.M., as they waited on Panther Key for the emergency helicopter, the woman who had loved so tenderly only a few days before died in Hawker's arms.

"I'm sorry, Hawk," Mellor whispered, filled with hurt and disgusted with himself. "I wouldn't have fired if she hadn't fired first. She would have killed you."

He and Mellor sat side by side in the darkness. Logan groaned, still breathing.

"I know," Hawker lied. "I know."

A mile offshore there was a burst of white light, then a thunderous vibration as *Demonio Del Mar* exploded, shooting debris three hundred feet into the night sky.

"Christ," whispered Graeme Mellor. "How am I going to explain all this to the FBI? How am I going to explain robbing a briefcase full of Colombian money from four guys who want to kill me, then using a damn Stinger missile to blow away their boat? I've got two choices, Hawk. I can spend the next two years testifying before congressional committees and doing paper-work, or I can lie."

The fiery white glow of the burning ship illuminated the island like summer moonlight. Hawker studied the perfect face of the Indian woman on his lap. It was as if she were sleeping.

"Tell the lie," said James Hawker softly. "Sometimes the lie is easier . . ."

EPILOGUE

James Hawker sat in a rich red leather chair in Jacob Montgomery Hayes's den.

Snow floated past the window, collecting on white trees and the silver expanse of Lake Michigan beyond the rolling estate.

Hayes wore his wine-color smoking jacket and had a pipe clenched between his teeth. He was holding his hands out toward the fireplace.

"I'm glad you came, James. I'm glad you finally decided you wanted to talk about it." He looked up and smiled. "By the way, Buck Hamilton called and said things have never been better on Mahogany Key. *Field and Stream* did a big piece on the Tarpon Inn, and business is booming." Hayes turned once more to the fire. "I didn't tell him you made me use the four hundred thousand dollars in Colombian currency to pay off the debt. As far as I'm concerned, neither one of you owed me any money in the first place."

Hawker sat for a long silent minute, studying the man before him. Finally he spoke. "You set me up, Jacob. You knew damn well that it was all connected. You knew what they were doing."

"Counterfeiting?" He shook his head. "I had no idea."

"But you knew that Guillermo's operation was responsible for the murder of your son. I figure they tried to buy some of your holdings in South America, or maybe even here in the United States. It was a coincidence that they happened to be working on an island where you used to fish, but you soon put two and two together. And you used me to take revenge."

Hayes thought for a moment, relighting the pipe. He exhaled fragrant smoke and nodded. "All true," he said. "I used you."

Hawker smacked his fist into his hand. "Then that business about working together on a vigilante operation—"

"I meant it!" Hayes said sharply. He sat forward in his chair, his face intense. "Certainly I used you, James. They had killed my son, for God's sake! Have you any idea what that means to a father? But I do want to go ahead—if you'll still have me. Don't you understand? The line between terrorism and vigilante work—the kind of important vigilante work we want to do—is a very fine line indeed. Your police record told me that you were tough enough. But I had to find out if you were smart enough and, more important, *compassionate* enough."

"It was a test."

"You're damn right it was a test!" Hayes sighed, and a light smile settled on his face. "If I was wrong to test you, I'm sorry. But I felt it was something I had to do. The big question is, did I pass James Hawker's test?" The husky older man stood and held out his hand. "Well, did I?"

Hawker hesitated. But not for long. There was something in Hayes's shrewd gray eyes that told him there would be no more tests, only trust and honesty from now on.

"What the hell." Hawker smiled. "We've still got a deal—"

He was interrupted as the door swung open and Hendricks, the butler, entered, pushing Logan in a wheelchair. Logan's face was red, as if he was angry, and it grew redder as he got shakily to his feet. He jerked a thumb over his shoulder, saying, "Hey, Hank here says I'm not allowed in the kitchen—"

"Hendricks, sir, *Hendricks*," said the butler, his expression pained.

"Hey, Hawk, tell him what a great cook I am!"

"Mr. Logan," the butler explained curtly, "was attempting to bake a pompano in—of all things—a brown paper bag—"

"Pompano?" asked Hawker.

"Baked in a bag?" asked Hayes, wetting his lips.

Logan watched triumphantly as the two men headed quickly toward the dining room. He sat back heavily in the wheelchair. "To the kitchen, Hendricks!" he said jauntily. And as an aside, he said over his shoulder, "I only have to stay in this contraption for two more weeks, Hank. Plenty of time, though, for me to show you all the little tricks of cooking."

"Wonderful," Hendricks said with a sniff, wheeling him toward dinner. "One can hardly wait . . ."

ABOUT THE AUTHOR

Randy Wayne White was born in Ashland, Ohio, in 1950. Best known for his series featuring retired NSA agent Doc Ford, he has published over twenty crime fiction and nonfiction adventure books. White began writing fiction while working as a fishing guide in Florida, where most of his books are set. His earlier writings include the Hawker series, which he published under the pen name Carl Ramm. White has received several awards for his fiction, and his novels have been featured on the *New York Times* bestseller list. He was a monthly columnist for *Outside* magazine and has contributed to several other publications, as well as lectured throughout the United States and travelled extensively. White currently lives on Pine Island in South Florida, and remains an active member of the community through his involvement with local civic affairs as well as the restaurant Doc Ford's Sanibel Rum Bar and Grill.

HAWKER EBOOKS

FROM OPEN ROAD MEDIA

Available wherever ebooks are sold

OPEN ROAD

INTEGRATED MEDIA

Open Road Integrated Media is a digital publisher and multimedia content company. Open Road creates connections between authors and their audiences by marketing its ebooks through a new proprietary online platform, which uses premium video content and social media.

Videos, Archival Documents, and New Releases

Sign up for the Open Road Media newsletter and get news delivered straight to your inbox.

Sign up now at
www.openroadmedia.com/newsletters